THE DARK WIND

BOOKS BY TONY HILLERMAN

Fiction

THE DARK WIND

PEOPLE OF DARKNESS

LISTENING WOMAN

DANCE HALL OF THE DEAD

THE FLY ON THE WALL

THE BLESSING WAY

THE BOY WHO MADE DRAGONFLY (for children)

Nonfiction

THE GREAT TAOS BANK ROBBERY

RIO GRANDE

NEW MEXICO

THE SPELL OF NEW MEXICO

THE
DARK
WIND

TONY HILLERMAN

1817

HARPER & ROW, PUBLISHERS, New York
Cambridge, Philadelphia, San Francisco,
London, Mexico City, São Paulo, Sydney

FIRST EDITION

Designer: Susan Hull

Library of Congress Cataloging in Publication Data

Hillerman, Tony.
  The dark wind.

  1. Navaho Indians—Fiction. I. Title.
PS3558.I45D3 1982   813'.54   81–47793
ISBN 0–06–014936–1   AACR2

82 83 84 85 86 10 9 8 7 6 5 4 3 2 1

This book is dedicated to the good people of Coyote Canyon, Navajo Mountain, Littlewater, Two Gray Hills, Heart Butte, and Borrego Pass, and most of all to those who are being uprooted from their ancestral homes in the Navajo-Hopi Joint Use country.

AUTHOR'S NOTES

The reader should be aware that I make no claims to being an authority on Hopi theology. Like Jim Chee of the Navajo Tribal Police, I am an outsider on the Hopi Mesas. I know only what one learns from long and respectful interest, and suggest that any of you who wish to learn more of the complex Hopi metaphysics turn to more knowledgeable writers. I particularly recommend *The Book of the Hopi* by my good friend Frank Waters.

The liturgical year of the Hopi religion is divided into seasonal halves which are more or less mirror images and which involve an elaborate calendar of ritual observances. These include the events which provide some of the background for this novel, but the calendar I use is not accurate.

Time has been even crueler to the village of Sityatki than is suggested herein. It was abandoned long ago and sand has drifted over what remains of its ruins.

All characters in this book are products of my imagination. None is based in any way on any living person.

THE DARK WIND

1

The Flute Clan boy was the first to see it. He stopped and stared.

"Somebody lost a boot," he said.

Even from where he stood, at least fifteen yards farther down the trail, Albert Lomatewa could see that nobody had lost the boot. The boot had been placed, not dropped. It rested upright, squarely in the middle of the path, its pointed toe aimed toward them. Obviously someone had put it there. And now, just beyond a dead growth of rabbit brush which crowded the trail, Lomatewa saw the top of a second boot. Yesterday when they had come this way no boots had been here.

Albert Lomatewa was the Messenger. He was in charge. Eddie Tuvi and the Flute Clan boy would do exactly what he told them.

"Stay away from it," Lomatewa said. "Stay right here."

He lifted the heavy pack of spruce boughs from his back and placed it reverently beside the path. Then he walked to the boot. It was fairly new, made of brown leather, with a flower pattern stitched into it and a curved cowboy heel. Lomatewa glanced past the rabbit brush at the second boot. It matched. Beyond the second boot, the path curved sharply around a weathered granite boulder. Lomatewa sucked in his breath. Jutting from behind the boulder he could see the bottom of a foot. The foot was bare and even from where

Lomatewa stood he could see there was something terribly wrong with it.

Lomatewa looked back at the two his kiva had sent to guard him on this pilgrimage for spruce. They stood where he had told them to stand—Tuvi's face impassive, the boy's betraying his excited curiosity.

"Stay there," he ordered. "There is someone here and I must see about it."

The man was on his side, legs bent stiffly, left arm stretched rigidly forward, right arm flexed upward with the palm resting beside his ear. He wore blue jeans, a jean jacket, and a blue-and-white-checked shirt, its sleeves rolled to the elbows. But it was a little while before Lomatewa noticed what the man was wearing. He was staring at his feet. The soles of both of them had been cut away. The bottom of the socks had been cut and the socks pushed up around the ankles, where they formed ragged white cuffs. Then the heel pads, and the pads at the balls of the feet, and the undertips of the toes had been sliced away. Lomatewa had nine grandchildren, and one great-grandchild, and had lived long enough to see many things, but he had never seen this before. He sucked in his breath, exhaled it, and glanced up at the hands. He expected to find them flayed, too. And he did. The skin had been sliced from them just as it had been from the feet. Only then did Lomatewa look at the man's face.

He had been young. Not a Hopi. A Navajo. At least part Navajo. There was a small, black-rimmed hole above his right eye.

Lomatewa stood looking down at the man, thinking how this would have to be handled. It had to be handled so that it would not interfere with the Niman Kachina. The sun was hot on him here, even though it was still early morning, and the smell of dust was in his nostrils. Dust, always dust. Reminding him of why nothing must interfere with the cere-

2

monial. For almost a year the blessing of rain had been with-drawn. He had thinned his corn three times, and still what little was left was stunted and withering in the endless drought. The springs were drying. There was no grass left for the horses. The Niman Kachina must be properly done. He turned and walked back to where his guardians were waiting.

"A dead Tavasuh," he said. Literally the word meant "head-pounder." It was a term of contempt which Hopis sometimes used for Navajos and Lomatewa chose it deliber-ately to set the tone for what he must do.

"What happened to his foot?" the Flute Clan boy asked. "The bottom was cut off his foot."

"Put down the spruce," Lomatewa said. "Sit down. We must talk about this." He wasn't worried about Tuvi. Tuvi was a valuable man in the Antelope Kiva and a member of the One Horn Society—a prayerful man. But the Flute Clan boy was still a boy. He said nothing more, though, simply sitting on the path beside his spruce bundle. The questions remained in his eyes. Let him wait, Lomatewa thought. Let him learn patience.

"Three times Sotuknang has destroyed the world," Loma-tewa began. "He destroyed the First World with fire. He destroyed the Second World with ice. He destroyed the Third World with flood. Each time he destroyed the world because his people failed to do what he told them to do." Lomatewa kept his eyes on the Flute Clan boy as he talked. The boy was his only worry. The boy had gone to school at Flagstaff and he had a job with the post office. There was talk that he did not plant his corn patches properly, that he did not properly know his role in the Kachina Society. Tuvi could be counted on but the boy must be taught. Loma-tewa spoke directly to him, and the boy listened as if he had not heard the old story a thousand times before.

"Sotuknang destroyed the world because the Hopis forgot

3

to do their duty. They forgot the songs that must be sung, the *pahos* that must be offered, the ceremonials that must be danced. Each time the world became infected with evil, people quarreled all the time. People became *powaqas*, and practiced witchcraft against one another. The Hopis left the proper Road of Life and only a few were left doing their duty in the kivas. And each time, Sotuknang gave the Hopis warning. He held back the rain so his people would know his displeasure. But everybody ignored the rainless seasons. They kept going after money, and quarreling, and gossiping, and forgetting the way of the Road of Life. And each time Sotuknang decided that the world had used up its string, and he saved a few of the best Hopis, and then he destroyed all the rest."

Lomatewa stared into the eyes of the Flute Clan boy. "You understand all this?"

"I understand," the boy said.

"We must do the Niman Kachina right this summer," Lomatewa said. "Sotuknang has warned us. Our corn dies in the fields. There is no grass. The wells are drying out. When we call the clouds, they no longer hear us. If we do the Niman Kachina wrong, Sotuknang will have no more patience. He will destroy the Fourth World."

Lomatewa glanced at Tuvi. His face was inscrutable. Then he spoke directly to the boy again. "Very soon it will be time for the kachinas to leave this Earth Surface World and go back to their home in the San Francisco Peaks. When we deliver this spruce back to our kivas, it will be used to prepare for the Going Home Dances to honor them. For days it will be very busy in the kivas. The prayers to be planned. The *pahos* to be made. Everything to be done exactly in the proper way." Lomatewa paused, allowing silence to make the effect he wanted. "Everybody thinking in the proper way," he added. "But if we report this body, this dead Navajo, to the police, nothing can be done right.

4

The police will come, the *bahana* police, to ask us questions. They will call us ousm Sothe kivas. Everything will be interrupted. Everybody will be thinking about the wrong things. They will be thinking of death and anger when they would be thinking only holy thoughts. The Niman Kachina will be messed up. The Going Home Dances would not be done right. Nobody would be praying."

He stopped again, staring at the Flute Clan boy.

"If you were the Messenger, what would you do?"

"I would not tell the police," the boy said.

"Would you talk of this in the kiva?"

"I would not talk of it."

"You saw the feet of the Navajo," Lomatewa said. "Do you know what that means?"

"The skin being cut away?"

"Yes. Do you know what it means?"

The Flute Clan boy looked down at his hands. "I know," he said.

"If you talk about that, it would be the worst thing of all. People would be thinking of evil just when they should be thinking of good."

"I won't talk about it," the boy said.

"Not until after the Niman dances," Lomatewa said. "Not until after the ceremonial is over and the kachinas are gone. After that you can tell about it."

Lomatewa picked up his bundle of spruce and settled the straps over his shoulders, flinching at the soreness in his joints. He felt every one of his seventy-three years, and he still had almost thirty miles to walk across Wepo Wash and then the long climb up the cliffs of Third Mesa. He led his guardians down the path past the body. Why not? They had already seen the mutilated feet and knew the meaning of that. And this death had nothing to do with the Hopis. This particular piece of evil was Navajo and the Navajos would have to pay for it.

2

◆

Just as he reached the rim of Balakai Mesa, Pauling checked the chronometer. It was 3:20:15. On time and on course. He held the Cessna about two hundred feet above the ground and the same distance below the top of the rimrock. Ahead, the moon hung yellow and slightly lopsided just above the horizon. It lit the face of the man who sat in the passenger's seat, giving his skin a waxy look. The man was staring straight ahead, lower lip caught between his teeth, studying the moon. To Pauling's right, not a hundred yards off the wingtip, the mesa wall rushed past—a pattern of black shadows alternating with reflected moonlight. It gave Pauling a sense of speed, oddly unusual in flight, and he savored it.

On the desert floor below, the sound of the engine would be echoing off the cliffs. But there was no one to hear it. No one for miles. He had chosen the route himself, flown it twice by daylight and once by night, memorized the landmarks and the terrain. There was no genuine safety in this business, but this was as safe as Pauling could make it. Here, for example, Balakai Mesa protected him from the radar scanners at Albuquerque and Salt Lake. Ahead, just to the left of the setting moon, Low Mountain rose to 6,700 feet and beyond that Little Black Spot Mesa was even higher. Southward, blocking radar from Phoenix, the high mass of Black Mesa extended for a hundred miles or more. All the way from the landing strip in Chihuahua there was less than a hundred miles where radar could follow him. It was a good route. He'd enjoyed finding it, and he loved flying it low, with its landmarks rising into the dying moon out of an infinity of darkness. Pauling savored the danger, the competition, as much as he delighted in the speed and the sense of being the controlling brain of a fine machine.

Balakai Mesa was behind him now and the black shape of Low Mountain slid across the yellow disk of the moon. In the darkness he could see a single sharp diamond of light— the single bulb which lit the gasoline pump at Low Mountain Trading Post. He banked the Cessna slightly to the left, following the course of Tse Chizzi Wash, skirting away from the place where the sound of his engine might awaken a sleeper.

"About there?" the passenger asked.

"Just about," Pauling said. "Over this ridge ahead there's Oraibi Wash, and then another bunch of ridges, and then you get to Wepo Wash. That's where we're landing. Maybe another six or seven minutes."

"Lonely country," the passenger said. He looked down upon it out of the side window, and shook his head. "Nobody. Like there was nobody else on the planet."

"Not many. Just a few Indians here and there. That's why it was picked."

The passenger was staring at the moon again. "This is the part that makes you nervous," he said.

"Yeah," Pauling agreed. But what part of "this part" did the man mean? Landing in the dark? Or what was waiting when they landed? For once Pauling found himself wishing he knew a little more about what was going on. He thought he could guess most of it. Obviously they weren't flying pot. Whatever was in the suitcases would have to be immensely valuable to warrant all the time and the special care. Picking this special landing place, for example, and having a passenger along. He hadn't had anyone riding shotgun with him for years. And when he had, when he'd first moved into this business—cut off from flying for Eastern by the bad reading on his heart—the passenger had been just one of the other hired hands sent along to make sure he didn't steal the load. This time the passenger was a stranger. He'd driven up to the motel at Sabinas Hidalgo with the boss just before it was time to go to the landing strip. Pauling guessed he must represent whoever was buying the shipment. The boss had said that Jansen would be at the other end, at the landing point with the buyers. "Two flashes, then a pause, and then two flashes," the boss had said. "If you don't see it, you don't land." Jansen representing the boss, and this stranger representing the buyers. Both trusted. It occurred to Pauling that the passenger, like Jansen, was probably a relative. Son or brother, or something like that. Family. Who else could you trust in this business, or in anything else?

Oraibi Wash flashed under them, a crooked streak of shadowed blackness in the slanting moonlight. Pauling eased the wheel slightly backward to move the aircraft up the desert slope, and then forward as the land fell away again. Broken ground under him now, a landscape cut by scores of little watercourses draining Black Mesa's flash floods into Wepo Wash. He had the engine throttled down to just above stalling speed now. To his left front he saw the black upthrust of basalt which was the right landmark shape in the right place. And then, just under his wingtip, there was the windmill, with the shadowed bottom of the wash curving just ahead. He should see the lights now. He should see Jansen blinking his . . . Then he saw them. A line of a dozen points of yellow light—the lenses of battery lanterns pointing toward him. And almost instantly, two flashes of white light, and two more flashes. Jansen's signal that all was well.

He made a slow pass over the lights and began a slow

circle, remembering exactly how the wash bottom looked as his wheels approached it, concentrating on making his memory replace the darkness with daylight.

Pauling became conscious that the passenger was staring at him. "Is that all you have?" the passenger asked. "You land by that goddamn row of flashlights?"

"The idea is not to attract any attention," Pauling said. Even in the dim light, he could see the passenger's expression was startled.

"You've done this before?" the man asked. His voice squeaked a little. "Just put it down blind in the dark like this?"

"Just a time or two," Pauling said. "Just when you have to." But he wanted to reassure the man. "Used to be in the Tactical Air Force. We had to practice landing those transport planes in the dark. But we're not really landing blind here. We have those lights."

They were lined up on the lights now. Pauling trimmed the plane. Wheels down. Flaps down. His memory gave him the arroyo bottom now. Nose up. He felt the lift going mushy under the wings, the passenger bracing himself in the seat beside him, that brief moment before touchdown when the plane was falling rather than flying.

"You do this on trust," the passenger said. "Jesus. Jesus." It was a prayer.

They were below the level of the wash banks now, the lights rushing toward them. The wheels touched with a jounce and a squeal as Pauling touched the brakes. Perfect, he thought. You have to learn to trust. And in the very split second that he had the thought, he saw that trust was a terrible mistake.

3

♦

At first Jim Chee ignored the sound of the plane. Something had moved beyond Windmill Number 6. Moved, and moved again, making a small furtive sound which carried much farther than it should have in the predawn stillness. A half hour earlier he'd heard a car purring up the sandy bottom of Wepo Wash, stopping perhaps a mile downstream. This new sound suggested that whoever had driven it might now be approaching the windmill. Chee felt the excitement of the hunt rising in him. His mind rejected the intrusive hum of the aircraft engine. But the engine sound became impossible to ignore. The plane was low, barely a hundred feet off the ground, and moving on a path that would take it just west of the nest Chee had made for himself in a growth of stunted mesquite. It passed between Chee and the windmill, flying without navigation lights but so close that Chee could see reflections from the illumination inside the cabin. He memorized its shape—the high wing, the tall, straight rudder; the nose sloping down from the cabin windshield. The only reason he could think of for such a flight at such an hour would be smuggling. Narcotics probably. What else? The plane purred away toward Wepo Wash and the sinking moon, quickly vanishing in the night.

Chee turned his eyes, and his thoughts, back toward the windmill. The plane was none of his business. Navajo Tribal Policemen had absolutely no jurisdiction in a smuggling case, or in a narcotics case, or in anything involving the U.S. Drug Enforcement Agency or the white man's war against white man's crime. His business was the vandalism of Windmill Subunit 6, the steel frame of which loomed awkward and ugly against the stars about one hundred yards west of him and which, on the rare occasions when the breeze picked up on this still summer night, made metallic creaking sounds as its blades moved. The windmill was only about a year old, having been installed by the Office of Hopi Partitioned Land to provide water for Hopi families being resettled along Wepo Wash to replace evicted Navajo families. Two months after it was erected, someone had removed the bolts that secured it to its concrete footings and used a long rope and at least two horses to pull it over. Repairs took two months, and three days after they were completed—with the bolts now securely welded into place—it had been vandalized again. This time, a jack handle had been jammed down into the gearbox during a heavy breeze. This had provoked a complaint from the Office of Hopi Partitioned Land to the Joint Use Administration Office at Keams Canyon, which produced a telephone call to the FBI office at Flagstaff, which called the Bureau of Indian Affairs Law and Order Division, which called the Navajo Tribal Police Headquarters at Window Rock, which sent a letter to the Tuba City subagency office of the Navajo Tribal Police. The letter resulted in a memo, which landed on the desk of Jim Chee. The memo said: "See Largo."

Captain Largo had been behind his desk, sorting through a manila folder.

"Let's see now," Largo had said. "Where you stand on identifying that John Doe body up on Black Mesa?"

"We don't have anything new," Chee had said. And that, as Chee knew Captain Largo already knew, meant they had absolutely nothing at all.

"I mean the fellow somebody shot in the head, the one

with no billfold, no identification," Largo said, exactly as if the Tuba City subagency was dealing in wholesale numbers of unidentified victims, and not this single exasperating one.

"No progress," Chee said. "He doesn't match anyone reported missing. His clothing told us exactly zero. Nothing to go on. Nothing."

"Ah," Largo said. He shuffled through the folder again. "How about the burglary at the Burnt Water Trading Post? You doing any good on that one?"

"No, sir," Chee said. He kept the irritation out of his voice.

"The employee stole the pawn jewelry, but we can't get a trace on him? Is that the way it stands?"

"Yes, sir," Chee said.

"Musket, wasn't it?" Largo asked. "Joseph Musket. On parole from the New Mexico State Penitentiary at Santa Fe. Right? But the silver hasn't turned up sold anywhere. And nobody's seen anything of Musket?" Largo was eyeing him curiously. "That's right, isn't it? You staying on top of that one?"

"I am," Chee had said. That had been mid-summer, maybe six weeks after Chee's transfer from the Crownpoint subagency, and he didn't know how to read Captain Largo. Now summer was ending and he still didn't know.

"That's a funny one," Largo had said. He had frowned. "What the hell did he do with all the pawn goods? Why doesn't he try to sell it? And where'd he go? You think he's dead?"

The same questions had been nagging Chee ever since he'd gotten the case. He didn't have any answers.

Largo noticed that. He sighed; peered back into the folder. "How about bootlegging?" he asked without looking up. "Any luck nailing Priscilla Bisti?"

"Just one near miss," Chee said. "But she and her boys got all the wine out of the pickup before we got there. No way to prove it was theirs."

Largo was looking at him, lips pursed. Largo's hands were folded across his ample stomach. The thumbs waved up and down, patiently. "You going to have to be smart to catch old Priscilla." Largo nodded, agreeing with himself. "Smart," he repeated.

Chee said nothing.

"How about all that witchcraft gossip out around Black Mesa?" Largo asked. "Doing any good with that?"

"Nothing I can pin down," Chee said. "Seems to be more of it than's natural, and maybe it's because so many people are going to be uprooted and moved out to make room for the Hopis. Trouble is I'm still too new around here for anybody to be telling me anything about witches." He wanted to remind Largo of that. It wasn't fair of the captain to expect him, still a stranger, to learn anything about witches. The clans of the northwestern reservation didn't know him yet. As far as they knew, he might be a skinwalker himself.

Largo didn't comment on the explanation. He fished out another manila folder. "Maybe you'll have some luck on this one," he said. "Somebody doesn't like a windmill." He slipped a letter out of the folder and handed it to Chee.

Chee read what Window Rock reported, with half of his mind trying to analyze Largo. The way the Navajos calculate kinship, the captain was a relative through clan linkage. Chee's crucial "born to" clan was the Slow Talking Dinee of his mother, but his "born for" clan—the clan of his father— was the Bitter Water People. Largo was born to the Standing Rock Dinee, but was "born for" the Red Forehead Dinee, which was also the secondary "born for" clan of Chee's father. That made kinsmen. Distant kinsmen, true enough, but kinsmen in a culture that made family of first importance and responsibility to relatives the highest value. Chee read the letter and thought about kinship. But he was remembering how a paternal uncle had once cheated him on a used-refrigerator sale, and that the worst whipping he'd ever taken in the Two Gray Hills Boarding School was from a maternal cousin. He handed the letter back to Largo without any comment.

"Whenever there's any trouble out there in the Joint Use Reservation it's usually the Gishis," Largo said. "Them and maybe the Yazzie outfit." He paused, thinking about it. "Or the Begays," he added. "They're into a lot of trouble." He folded the letter back into the file and handed the file to Chee. "Could be just about anybody," he concluded. "Anyway, get it cleared up."

Chee took the folder. "Get it cleared up," he said.

Largo looked at him, his expression mild. "That's right," he said. "Can't have somebody screwing up that Hopi windmill. When the Hopis move onto our land, they got to have water for their cows."

"Got any other suggestions about suspects?"

Largo pursed his lips. "We have to move about nine thousand Navajos off that Joint Use land," he said. "I'd say you could cut it down to about nine thousand suspects."

"Thanks," Chee said.

"Glad to help," Largo said. "You take it from there and get it narrowed down to one." He grinned, showing crooked white teeth. "That'll be your job. Narrow it down to one and catch him."

Which was exactly what Chee had been spending this long night trying to do. The plane was gone now, and if anything stirred around the windmill, Chee could neither see nor hear it. He yawned, unholstered his pistol, and used its barrel to scratch an otherwise unreachable place between his shoulder blades. The moon was down and the stars blazed without competition in a black sky. It was suddenly colder. Chee picked up the blanket, untangled it from the mesquite, and draped it around his shoulders. He thought about the windmill, and the sort of malice involved in vandalizing it,

14

and why the vandal didn't spread his attentions among windmills 1 through 8, and then he thought about the perplexing affair of Joseph Musket, who had stolen maybe seventy-five pounds of silver concha belts, squash blossom necklaces, bracelets, and assorted pawn silver, and then done absolutely nothing with the loot. Chee had already worked the puzzle of Joseph Musket over in his mind so often that all the corners were worn smooth. He worked it over again, looking for something overlooked.

Why had Jake West hired Musket? Because he was a friend of West's son. Why had West fired him? Because he had suspected Musket of stealing. That made sense. And then Musket came back to the Burnt Water Trading Post the night after he was fired and looted its storeroom of pawned jewelry. That, too, made sense. But stolen jewelry always turned up. It was given to girl friends. It was sold. It was pawned at other trading posts, or in Albuquerque, or Phoenix, or Durango, or Farmington, or any of those places surrounding the reservation which traded in jewelry. It was so logical, inevitable, predictable, that police all through the Southwest had a standard procedure for working such cases. They posted descriptions, and waited. And when the jewelry started turning up, they worked back from that. Why hadn't the inevitable happened this time? What was different about Musket? Chee considered what little Musket's parole officer had been able to tell him about the man. Even his nickname was an enigma. Ironfingers. Navajos tended to match such labels with personal characteristics, calling a slim girl Slim Girl or a man with a thin mustache Little Whiskers. What would cause a young man to be called Ironfingers? More important, was he still alive? Largo had asked that, too. If he was dead, that would explain everything.

Except why he was dead.

Chee sighed, and wrapped the blanket around his shoulders, and found himself thinking of another of his unresolved cases. John Doe: cause of death, gunshot wound in the temple. Size of bullet, .38 caliber. Size of John Doe, five feet, seven inches. Weight of John Doe, probably 155 pounds, based on what was left of him when Chee and Cowboy Dashee brought him in. Identity of John Doe? Who the hell knows? Probably Navajo. Probably mature young adult. Certainly male. He had been Chee's introduction to duty in the Tuba City district. His first day after his transfer from Crownpoint. "Go out and learn the territory," Largo had said, but a few miles west of Moenkopi the dispatcher had turned him around and sent him into Joint Use country. "Subject at Burnt Water Trading Post has information about a body," the dispatcher said. "See Deputy Sherfiff Dashee. He'll meet you there."

"What's the deal?" Chee had asked. "Isn't that outside our territory now?"

The dispatcher hadn't known the answer to that, but when he got to the Burnt Water Trading Post and met Deputy Sheriff Albert (Cowboy) Dashee, the deputy had the answer.

"The stiff's a Navajo," he explained. "That's what we hear. Somebody's supposed to have shot him, so somebody figured one of you guys ought to go along." When they had finally got to the body it was hard to imagine how anyone had guessed his tribe, or even his sex. Decay was advanced. Scavengers had found the body—animal, bird, and insect. What was left was mostly a tattered ragbag of bare bone, sinew, gristle, and a little hard muscle. They had looked at it awhile, and wondered why the boots had been removed and left on the path, and made a fruitless search for anything that would identify the man, or explain the bullet hole in his skull. And then Cowboy Dashee had done something friendly.

He'd unrolled the body bag they'd carried along and when Chee had bent to help him, he'd waved Chee away.

"We Hopis have our hang-ups," he said, "but we don't

16

have the trouble you Navajos got with handling dead bodies." And so Dashee had tucked John Doe into the body bag while Chee watched. That left nothing to do but discover who he'd been, and who had killed him, and why he took off his boots before they did it.

A sound from a long way off brought Chee back to the present. It came from about where the car had stopped down in the wash—the sound of metal striking metal, perhaps, but too dim and distant to identify. And then he heard the plane again. This time it was south of him, moving eastward. Apparently it had circled. The moonset had left a bright orange glow outlining the ridge of Big Mountain. For a moment the plane was high enough to reflect moonlight from a wing. It was turning. Completing a circle. Once again it came almost directly toward him, sinking out of the moonlight and down into the darkness. Chee heard a clanking sound over the low purr of the engine. The wheels being lowered? It was too dark to tell. The plane passed within two hundred yards of him, downhill and not much above eye level. It flew just above Wepo Wash and then it disappeared.

Abruptly the purr of the engine stopped. Chee frowned. Had the pilot cut the engine? No. He heard it again, muted now.

It takes about five seconds for sound to travel a mile. Even after a mile, after five seconds of dilution by distance, the sound reached Chee's ear like a thunderclap. Like an explosion. Like tons of metal striking stone.

There was silence again for a second or two, perhaps even three. And then a single sharp snapping sound, from a mile away but instantly identifiable. The sound of a gunshot.

4

The raw smell of gasoline reached Jimmy Chee's nostrils. He stopped, aiming the flashlight down the arroyo ahead of him, looking for the source and regaining his breath. He'd covered the distance from his clump of mesquite in less than fifteen minutes, running when the terrain permitted it, scrambling up and down the dry watercourses, dodging through the brush and cactus, keeping the glow of the setting moon to his left front. Once, just before he had reached the cliff edge of Wepo Wash, he had heard the grind of a starter, an engine springing to life, and the receding sound of a vehicle moving down the dry watercourse away from him. He had seen a glow where the vehicle's lights had reflected briefly off the arroyo wall. He'd seen nothing else. Now the flashlight beam reflected from metal, and beyond the metal, more metal in a tangled mass. Chee stood inspecting what the light showed him. Over the sound of his labored breathing, he heard something. Falling dirt. Someone had scrambled up the cliff and out of the wash. He flicked the light beam toward the noise. It picked up a residue of dust, but no movement. Whatever had dislodged the earth was out of sight.

Cautiously now, Chee walked to the wreckage.

The plane's left wing had apparently struck first, slamming into a great outcrop of rock which had forced the wash into an abrupt northward detour. Part of the wing had torn off, and the force had pivoted the plane, slamming its fuselage into the rock at about a forty-five degree angle. Chee's flash reflected from an unbroken cabin window. He peered through it. His light struck the side of the head of a man with curly blond hair. The head was bowed forward as if the man were sleeping. No sign of blood. But lower, the front of the cabin had been crushed backward. Where the man's chest had been, there was metal. Beyond this, Chee could see a second man, in the pilot's seat. Dark hair with gray in it. Blood on the face. Movement!

Chee ducked through the torn gap in the aluminum where the cabin door had been, forced a bent passenger seat out of the way, and reached the pilot. The man was still breathing, or seemed to be. Chee, squatting awkwardly amid the torn metal, reached forward and unfastened the pilot's safety belt. It was wet and warm with blood. He eased himself between the seats, far enough forward to examine the pilot in the light of his flash. The man had bled copiously from a tear on the right side of his neck—a ragged gash which now barely seeped. It was too late for a tourniquet. The heart had run out of anything to pump.

Chee sat back on his heels and assessed the situation. The pilot was dying. If this cramped space were an operating room with a surgeon at work and blood being pumped back into the pilot, the man might have a chance. But Chee was helpless to save him.

Yet there's the human urge to do something. Chee eased the man out of the pilot's seat and slid the limp form between the seats and out of the torn cabin. He laid the pilot carefully, face up, on the packed sand. He took the pilot's wrist and felt for a pulse. There was none. Chee switched off his flashlight.

With the moon down, at the bottom of Wepo Wash the darkness was total. Overhead, freed now from competition with the moon, a billion stars blazed against black space.

The pilot no longer existed. His *chindi* had slipped away to wander in the darkness—one more ghost to infect the People with sickness and make the nights dangerous. But Chee had come to terms with ghosts long ago when he was a teenager in boarding school.

He gave his eyes time to adjust to the darkness. At first there was only the line of the clifftop, which separated the starscape from the black. Gradually forms took shape. The upthrust surviving wing of the plane, the shape of the basalt outcrop which had destroyed it. Chee felt cold against the skin of his hands. He put them into his jacket pockets. He walked to the outcrop and around it, thinking. He thought of the car he had heard driving away and of the person, or persons, who must be in it. Persons who had walked away from the pilot and left the man to die alone in the dark. Now the starlight gave the canyon shape, defining a difference between its sandy bottom and its walls, even suggesting brush at the base of its cliffs. It was absolutely windless now, utterly silent. Chee leaned his hip against the basalt, fished out a cigaret and a kitchen match.

He struck the match against the stone. It made a great flare of yellow light which illuminated the gray-yellow sand around his feet, the slick black of the basalt, and the white shirtfront of a man. The man sat on the sand, legs outthrust, and the quick flare of the sulfur flame reflected from the lenses of his eyeglasses.

Chee dropped the match, stepped back, and fumbled out his flashlight. The man was wearing a dark-gray business suit with a vest and a neatly knotted blue necktie. His feet had slid from under him, leaving heel tracks in the sand and pulling up his trouser legs, so that white skin was bared above the top of black socks. In the yellow beam of Chee's flash he looked perhaps forty-five or fifty, but death and yellow light ages the face. His hands hung at his sides, resting on the sand. Between thumb and forefinger of his right hand he held a small white card. Chee knelt by the hand and focused his light on it. It was a card from the Hopi Cultural Center. Holding it by the edges, Chee slipped it out and turned it over. On the reverse side someone had written:

"If you want it back, check into here."

Chee slipped the card back between the fingers. This would be a federal case. Very much a federal case. None of this would be any of his business.

5

Captain Largo was standing at the wall map, making calculations.

"The plane's here," he said, punching a stubby finger against the paper. "And your car was parked here?" He touched the paper again. "Maybe two miles. Maybe less."

Chee said nothing. It had occurred to him about three questions back that something unusual was happening.

"And you called your first report in at twenty minutes after five," the man named Johnson said. "Say it takes forty minutes to walk to your car, that would leave another fifty minutes from the time you said the plane crashed." Johnson was a tall, lean, red-haired man, his face a mass of freckles. He wore black cowboy boots of some exotic leather, and denims. His pale mustache was well trimmed and his pale-blue eyes watched Chee. They had watched Chee since the moment he'd entered the office, with the impersonal unblinking stare policemen tend to develop. Chee reminded himself that it was one of several professional habits that he must try to avoid.

"Fifty minutes," Chee said. "Yeah. That sounds about right."

Silence. Largo studied the map. Johnson was sitting with his chair tilted back against the wall, his hands locked behind his head, staring at Chee. He shifted his weight, causing the chair to creak.

"Fifty minutes is a lot of time," Johnson said.

A lot of time for what? Chee thought. But he said nothing.

"You say before you got to the wreck you heard a car engine starting, or maybe it was a pickup truck, and somebody driving away. And then when you got there, you heard somebody climbing out of the wash behind the plane." Johnson's tone made the statement into a question.

"That's what I say," Chee said. He caught Largo glancing at him. Largo's face was full of thought.

"Our people turned in a report a lot like yours," Johnson said. "You don't count your own tracks, of course, so you were looking at four sets and they were looking at five. Someone climbing out of the wash, like you said." Johnson held up one finger. "And the smooth-soled, pointy-toed shoes of the stiff." Johnson held up a second finger. "And a set of waffle soles, and a set of cowboy boots." Two more fingers went up. "And the boot soles we now know were yours." Johnson added his thumb to complete the count at five. He stared at Chee, waiting for agreement.

"Right," Chee said, looking into Johnson's cold blue stare.

"It looked to our people—that's the FBI—that the cowboy-boot tracks stepped on your tracks some places, and in some places you stepped on them," Johnson said. "Same with the waffle soles."

Chee considered what Johnson had said for about five seconds.

"Which would mean that the three of us were there at the same time," Chee said.

"All together," Johnson said. "In a bunch."

Chee was thinking he'd just been accused of a crime. And then he thought that someone had once said a little knowledge is a dangerous thing, and how well that axiom applied to reading tracks. Trackers tend to forget that people step on their own footprints. It was something his uncle had taught him to watch for—and to read.

"Any comments on that?" Johnson asked.

"No," Chee said.

"You saying you weren't there at the same time as the other fellows?"

"Are you saying I was?" Chee said. "What you seem to be saying is that the FBI hasn't had much luck finding somebody who can read tracks."

Johnson's stare was totally unself-conscious. Chee looked into it, curious about the man. The face was hard, intelligent, grim—a confident face. Chee had seen the look often enough to recognize it. He'd seen it in the Hopi boy who'd set the Arizona High School cross-country track record at the Flagstaff marathons, and on the face of the rodeo cowboy who won the big belt at Window Rock, and elsewhere in people who were very, very good at what they were doing, and knew it, and let a sort of arrogant confidence show in the careless way they used their eyes. Chee's experience with federal cops had not left him with any illusions of their competence. But Johnson would be another matter altogether. If Chee were a criminal, he would not want Johnson hunting him.

"You're sticking to your report, then," Johnson said finally. "Anything you can add that would help us?"

"Help you what?" Chee asked. "Maybe I could help your man learn something about tracking."

Johnson let the chair legs hit the floor, unlocked his hands, and stood.

"Nice to meet you folks," he said. "And, Mr. Chee, I'll probably be talking to you again. You going to be around?"

"Most likely," Chee said.

The door closed behind Johnson. Largo was still examining the map.

"I can't tell you much about that," Largo said. "Just a little."

"You don't need to tell me much," Chee said. "I would

say that the narcs don't think it was a coincidence that I was out there by the wash when the plane landed. They think I was really out there to meet the plane and that me and waffle soles and cowboy boots hauled off the drug shipment—or whatever it was. Spent the missing fifty minutes loading the stuff. That about it?"

"Just about," Largo said mildly.

"There's more?"

"Nothing much," Largo said. "Nothing they exactly told me."

"But something that makes them suspicious of me?"

"Makes 'em suspicious of somebody local," Largo said. "I get an impression that the Drug Enforcement Agency don't think that shipment got hauled very far. They think it's hidden around there someplace close."

Chee frowned. "How would they know that?"

"How does the DEA know anything?" Largo asked. "I think they got about half of the drug smuggling industry on their payroll. Ratting for them."

"Seems like it," Chee said.

"And then they do a hell of a lot of guessing," Largo added.

"I noticed that, too," Chee said.

"Like about you helping haul away the shipment."

"You think that was a bad guess?"

"Most likely," Largo said.

"Thanks," Chee said. "Johnson tell you who was in the plane?"

"I gather the pilot was somebody they know. One of the regulars who flies stuff in from Mexico for one of the big outfits. Fellow named Pauling. I don't think they have an identification on the passenger yet. The guy on the ground, the guy who got shot, his name was Jerry Jansen. Lawyer from Houston. Supposed to be in the narcotics business."

"I didn't move him," Chee said. "Shot, was he?"

"In the back," Largo said.

"It looks simple enough," Chee said. "A plane's hauling in dope. Somebody comes in a vehicle to accept the delivery, right? Only the plane crashes. Two of the guys receiving the shipment decide to steal it. They shoot their partner in the back, leave a note to the owners, or maybe the buyers, to tell them how to make contact to buy their stuff back. Then they haul it away. Right? But the DEA doesn't seem to think the shipment got hauled out. They think it's hidden out there somewhere. Right?"

"That's what Johnson seemed to be thinking," Largo said.

"Now why would they think that?" Chee asked.

Largo was looking out his window. He seemed not to have heard the question. But finally he said, "I'd guess the DEA had this shipment wired. I think they had themselves an informer in the right place."

Chee nodded. "Yeah," he said. "But for some reason beyond the understanding of this poor Indian, the DEA didn't want to move in and grab the plane and arrest everyone."

Largo was still looking out the window. He glanced back at Chee. "Hell," he said. "Who knows. The feds work in strange and mysterious ways and they don't explain things to the Navajo Tribal Police." He grinned. "Especially they don't when they think maybe a Navajo Tribal Policeman got off with the evidence."

"Makes you curious," Chee said.

"It does," Largo said. "I think I'll do some asking around."

"I'm thinking about that card," Chee said. "That could be why the feds think the shipment's still around here. Why else would the hijacker do his dealing through the Hopi motel? Why not contact 'em in Houston, or wherever they operate?"

"I wondered when that was going to occur to you," Largo said. "If Jim Chee stole the shipment, he wouldn't know how to get in touch with the owners. So Jim Chee would leave a note telling them how to contact him."

"Thinking the press would report the note? Is that what I'd think? Wouldn't it occur to me that maybe the DEA would keep the note secret?"

"It might," Largo said. "But if you thought of that, you'd be smart enough to know they'd have lawyers nosing around. Whoever owned that plane has a legal, legitimate interest in that crash. They'd ask to see the investigating officer's report, and we'd show it to them. So Jim Chee would be sure to put what it said on the card in his report. Like you did."

Jim Chee, who actually hadn't thought of that at all, nodded. "Pretty slick of Jim Chee," he said.

"Got a call about forty-five minutes ago," Largo said. "From Window Rock. Your buddy did it again. To the windmill."

"Last night?" Chee's tone was incredulous. "After the crash?"

Largo shrugged. "Joint Use Office called Window Rock. All I know is somebody screwed up the machinery again and Window Rock wants it stopped."

Chee was speechless. He started for the door, then stopped. Largo was standing behind his desk, reading something in Chee's folder. He was a short man with the barrel-chested, hipless shape common among western Navajos, and his round face was placid as he read. Chee felt respect for him. He wasn't sure he would like him. Probably he wouldn't.

"Captain," he said.

Largo looked up.

"Johnson had trouble with that lost fifty minutes at the airplane. Do you?"

"I don't think so," Largo said. His expression was totally neutral. "I know something Johnson doesn't." He held up the folder. "I know how slow you work."

6

◆

Jake West was behind the counter explaining the ramifications of money orders to a teenaged Navajo girl who seemed to want to buy something out of the Sears catalog. West had acknowledged Chee's presence with a nod and a grin but had done nothing to hurry his dealings with his customer. Nor did Chee expect him to. He leaned against the metal of the frozen foods cabinet, and waited for West, and thought his thoughts, and listened to the three gossips who were talking about witches on the porch just outside the open door. The three were a middle-aged Navajo woman (a Gishi, Chee had deduced), an elderly Navajo woman, and an even older Navajo man, whom the younger woman had called Hosteen Yazzie. She was doing most of the talking, loudly for the benefit of a hard-of-hearing audience. The subject was witchcraft in the Black Mesa–Wepo Wash country. The witchcraft gossip sounded typical of what one expected to hear in a season of drought or hard times—and for the Joint Use Reservation Navajos this was indeed a season of hard times. The usual pattern. Somebody had been out at dusk hunting a ram and had seen a man lurking around, and the man had turned into an owl and flown away. One of the Gishi girls had heard her horses all excited and had gone out to see about it, and a dog had been bothering them, and she shot at the dog with her .22, and the dog had turned into a man and disappeared in the darkness.

An old man back on the mesa had heard sounds on the roof of his hogan during the night, and had seen something coming down through the smoke hole. Maybe it was dislodged dirt. Maybe it was corpse powder dropped by the witch. Chee's attention wandered. He heard Hosteen Yazzie say, "I guess the witch got the corpse powder from that man he killed," and then Chee was listening again, intently now. The Gishi woman said, "I guess so," and the conversation drifted away, to another day and another subject. Chee shifted his weight against the refrigerator case and considered the witch who had killed a man. If he walked through the door and asked Hosteen Yazzie to explain himself, he would meet only blank silence. These Navajos didn't know him. They'd never talk of witchcraft to a person who might be the very witch who was worrying them.

From across the store, West's laugh boomed out. He was leaning over the teenager now, his bulk making her seem a scaled-down model of a girl. He'd weigh 275 pounds, Chee guessed, maybe 300—some of it fat and some of it muscle, built on a barrel-like frame which made him seem short until he stood close to you. The laughter showed a great row of teeth through a curly beard. Where the beard and mustache didn't hide it, Jake West's face was a moonscape of pits and pockmarks. Only his forehead, revealed by a central baldness, was smooth—a placid lake of pink skin surrounded by a mass of graying curls.

Jim Chee had first met West when Chee was brand new in the district—the day they'd recovered John Doe's body. And the day after they'd brought the body in, the dispatcher had relayed a message to drop in at the Burnt Water store because West had something to tell him. The something hadn't been much—a little information which suggested the location one of the area's bootleggers might be using to deliver to his customers. But it was that day that Chee had seen, actually seen, Joseph Musket. It isn't often that a cop gets to see the burglar the day before the burglary.

Chee had parked in front, come in, seen West in his office in conversation with a young man wearing a red shirt. West had shouted something like "Be with you in a minute," and in a minute the young man had walked out of West's office and past Chee and out the front door. West stood at the office door, glaring after him.

"That son of a bitch," West had said. "I fired him."

"He didn't look like he cared much," Chee had said.

"I guess he didn't," West said. "I give him a job so he can qualify for parole and the bastard shows up for work whenever it damn well pleases him. And that ain't often. And I think he was stealing from me."

"Want to file a complaint?"

"Let it go," West said. "He used to be a friend of my son's. My boy wasn't ever good at picking friends."

And the very next morning, there'd been another call. Somebody had unlocked the storage room where West kept jewelry pawned by his customers, and walked out with about forty of the best pieces. Only West and Joseph Musket had access to the key. Since then Chee had learned a little about West. He'd operated the Burnt Water store for twenty years. He'd come from Phoenix, or Los Angeles, depending on your source, and he'd once been married to a Hopi woman, but no longer was. He'd had a son, maybe two, by a previous marriage, and had established a fairly good reputation, as reputations go among trading post operators. He was not on Captain Largo's list of known bootleggers, had never been nailed fencing stolen property, paid relatively fair prices for the jewelry he took in pawn and charged relatively fair interest rates, and seemed to get along well with both Navajo and Hopi customers. The Hopis, Chee had been told, considered him a *powaqa*—a "two-heart"—one of those persons in whom dwelled the soul of an animal as well as the soul of a human. This was the sophisticated Hopis' version of a witch. Chee had asked two Hopis he'd met about this rumor. One said it was nonsense—that only descendants of the Fog Clan could be two-hearts and that the Fog Clan was almost extinct among the Hopi villages. The other, an elderly woman, thought West might be a two-heart, but not much of one. Now West had collected his money from the Navajo girl and given her the money order.

He loomed down the counter toward Chee, teeth showing white through the beard in a huge grin.

"Officer Chee," he said, offering his hand. It engulfed Chee's hand, but the handshake, like the voice, was surprisingly gentle. "You're just a little bit late. I expected you five minutes ago." The grin had been converted to sternness.

Chee had seen West's playfulness before. He wasn't fooled. But he played along.

"How'd you know when I was coming?"

"Mind power," West said. "And because you Navajos won't believe in powers like that, I planted a thought in your mind so I could prove it to you." West stared down at Chee, his eyes fierce. "You are thinking of a card."

"Nope," Chee said.

"Yes you are," West insisted. "It's subconscious. You don't even know it yourself, but I planted the thought. Now quit wasting our time and tell me the card."

Chee found himself thinking of cards. A deck of cards spilled across a table. A bunch of spades. No particular card.

"Come on," West said. "Out with it."

"Three of diamonds," Chee said.

West's fierceness modified itself into smiling self-satisfaction. "Exactly right," he said. West wore blue-and-white-striped coveralls, large even for his bulk. He fished into one of their pockets. "And since you Navajos are such skeptical people, I arranged some proof for you." He handed Chee a small envelope of the sort used to mail notes and invitations.

"The three of diamonds," West said.

"Wonderful," Chee said. He noticed the envelope was sealed and put it in his shirt pocket.

"Aren't you going to open it?"

"I trust you," Chee said, "and I really came in to see if you can help me."

West's eyebrows rose. "You working on that plane crash? The drug business?"

"That's a federal case," Chee said. "FBI, Drug Enforcement Agency. We don't handle such things. I'm working on a vandalism case."

"That windmill," West said. He looked thoughtful. "Yes. That's a funny business."

"You been hearing anything?"

West laughed. "Naturally. Or I was. Now everybody's talking about the plane crash, and drug smuggling, and killing that guy—a lot more interesting than a vandalized windmill."

"But maybe not as important," Chee said.

West looked at him, thinking about that.

"Well, yes," he said. "From our point of view, yes. Depends on who gets killed, doesn't it?" He motioned Chee around behind the counter and led him through the doorway from store into living quarters. "They ought to kill them all," West said to the hallway in front of him. "Scum."

The West living room was long, narrow, cool, dark. Its thick stone walls were cut by four windows, but vines had grown so thickly over them that they let in only a green dimness. "Sit down," West said, and he lowered himself into a heavy plastic recliner. "We'll talk about windmills, and airplanes, and men who get themselves shot in the back."

Chee sat on the sofa. It was too soft for him and he sank into its lumpy upholstery. Such furniture always made him uneasy. "First we need to settle something," Chee said. "That fellow wrecking that windmill might be a friend of yours; or it could be that you think wrecking that windmill isn't such a bad idea under the circumstances. If that's the way it is, I'll go away and no hard feelings."

West was grinning. "Ah," he said. "I like the way your mind works. Why waste the talk? But the way it is, I don't know who's doing it, and I don't like vandalism, and worse than that, maybe it's going to lead to worse trouble and God knows we don't need any of that."

"Good," Chee said.

"Trouble is, the thing has me puzzled." West put his elbows on the armrests of the chair, made a tent of his fingers. "Common sense says one of your Navajo families is doing it. Who'd blame 'em? I guess the Gishi family has been living along that wash for four generations, or five, and the Yazzies something like that, and some others maybe as long. Toughing it out, hauling water in, and as soon as the federal court turns it over to the Hopis, the feds drill 'em a bunch of wells." West had been studying his fingers. Now he looked at Chee. "Sort of adds insult to the injury."

Chee said nothing. West was an old hand at communicating with Navajos. He would talk at his own pace until he said what he had to say, without expecting the social feedback of a white conversation.

"You got a few mean sons-a-bitches out there," West went on. "That's a fact. Get too much to drink in Eddie Gishi and he's a violent man. Couple of others as bad or worse. So maybe one of them would pull down a windmill." West examined his tented fingers while he considered the idea. "But I don't much.think they did."

Chee waited. West would explain himself when he had his thoughts sorted out. On the mantel of the stone fireplace behind West's chair a clutter of photographs stood in an uneven row: a good-natured-looking boy in Marine blues, the same boy in what Chee guessed was a blowup of a high school yearbook photograph, a picture of West himself in a tuxedo and a top hat, looking a great deal younger. All the other photographs included more than one person: West with a pretty young Hopi woman who was probably West's second wife, West and the same woman with the boy, the same trio with assorted persons whom Chee couldn't identify. None of the pictures looked new. They had collected dust—a sort of gallery out of a dead period from the past.

"I don't think they did," West continued finally, "because of the way they're acting. Lot of gossip about it, of course. Lots of talk." He looked up at Chee, wanting to explain. "You come from Crownpoint. Over in New Mexico. It's more settled around there. More people. More things to do. Out here, the nearest movie show's a hundred miles away in Flagstaff. Television reception's poor and most people don't have electricity anyway. Nothing much happens and nothing much to do. So if somebody pulls down a windmill, it breaks the monotony."

Chee nodded.

"You hear a lot of speculation. You know—guessing about who's doing it. The Hopis, they're sure they know. It's the Yazzies, or it's the Gishi bunch, or somebody. They're mad about it. And nervous. Wondering what will happen next. And the Navajos, they think it's sort of funny, some of them anyway, and they're guessing about who's doing it. Old Hosteen Nez, he'll say something speculative about a Yazzie boy, or Shirley Yazzie will make a remark about the Nezes being in the windmill-fixing business. So forth."

West took down his tent of fingers and leaned forward. "You hear a little of that from *everybody*." He stressed the word. "If one of the Navajos was doing it, I think they wouldn't be speculating. I think they'd be keeping quiet about it. That's the way I've got these Wepo Wash Navajos figured." West glanced at Chee, looking slightly embarrassed. "I've been living with these people twenty years," he said. "You get to know 'em."

34

"So who's breaking the windmill?" Chee asked. "Rule out us Navajos and that doesn't leave anybody but the Hopis, and you."

"It's not me," West said, grinning his great, irregular grin. "I got nothing against windmills. When all the Navajos get moved out of here, most of my customers are going to be Hopis. I'm in favor of them having all their windmills in good working order."

"Always the same mill," Chee said. "And over on the Gishi grazing permit. You'd think that would narrow it down to the Gishis."

"The *former* Gishi grazing permit," West corrected. "Now it's Hopi territory." He shook his head. "I don't think it's the Gishis. Old Emma Gishi runs that bunch. She's tough and you don't push her. But she's practical. Knocking down a windmill don't do her no good. She wouldn't do it out of meanness, and if Emma says don't do it, none of the Gishis does it. She runs that bunch like a railroad. You want a drink of something? I heard you don't drink whiskey."

"I don't," Chee said.

"How about coffee?"

"Always," Chee said.

"I'll mix up some instant," West said. "What I meant was she runs that bunch like they used to run railroads. Not like they run 'em now."

West disappeared through the doorway into what Chee presumed was the kitchen. Something clattered. Chee pulled the envelope out of his pocket and inspected it. A perfectly plain white envelope without a mark on it. Inside he could see the shape of a playing card. He was absolutely certain it would be the three of diamonds. How had West done that? Chee felt faintly guilty. He shouldn't have denied West the pleasure of seeing the finale of the trick. He slipped the card back into the pocket of his uniform shirt and examined the room. Three Navajo rugs, two of them fine examples of collector-quality Two Gray Hills weaving. An old dark-stained bookcase along the wall away from the windows held a few books and a gallery of kachina figures. Chee recognized Masaw, the guardian spirit of this Fourth World of the Hopis, and the god of fire and death, and the lord of Hell. It was a beautiful job, almost a foot tall and probably worth a thousand dollars. Most of the other kachinas were also Hopi, but the Zuni Shalako figures were there, and the Zuni Longhorn spirit, and two grotesque members of the Mudhead fraternity. All good, but Masaw was clearly the feature of the collection. It held a torch and its face was the traditional blood-spotted mask.

West reappeared in the doorway, bearing mugs. "Hope it's hot enough. I didn't let the water boil."

Chee sipped. The coffee was one stage past lukewarm and tasted muddy. "Fine," he said.

"Now," West said, easing himself back into the recliner. "We have talked about windmills. Now we talk a little about airplane crashes and dead gangsters."

Chee took another sip.

"From what was in the paper, and on TV last night, and what dribbles in from here and there, I get the impression that somebody got off with the shipment."

"That seems to be what the feds are thinking," Chee said.

"Two men killed in the plane crash," West said. "A third man shot and left sitting there with a message in his hand. So the DEA figures the dope got hijacked. Right?"

"I'll bet you know as much about it as I do," Chee said. "Maybe more. It's not our jurisdiction."

West ignored that. "From what I hear, you fellows figure the dope is hidden back in there someplace. That whoever got off with it didn't haul it away with him?"

Chee shrugged. West waited expectantly. "Well," Chee said finally, "I do get that kind of impression. Don't ask me why."

"Why wouldn't it be hauled out?" West asked. "They came in there to haul it off. Why not haul it off? Where would they hide it? How big is it?"

"I don't know," Chee said. "You thinking about finding it?"

West's huge grin split his beard. "Wouldn't that be fine? To find something like that. It'd be worth a fortune. They say it's cocaine, and that stuff sells for thousands of dollars an ounce. I heard the pure stuff would bring five hundred thousand dollars a pound, time you dilute it down and sell it to the customer."

"Where you going to find a buyer?"

"There's a will, there's a way," West said. He finished his coffee, put down the cup, grimaced. "Terrible-tasting stuff," he said. "How about the pilot? Somebody said he was still alive when you got there."

"Just barely," Chee said. "Who is this somebody that's telling you all this?"

West laughed. "You're forgetting the first rule of collecting gossip. You never tell anybody who told you, or they stop telling."

Probably Cowboy Dashee, Chee thought. Cowboy was a talker, and it was the sort of information he'd have. But a half-dozen various kinds of cops would have been through the trading post since the crash. It could have been any of them, or it could have been second or third hand, or it could just be an educated guess.

West changed the subject. Had any of his stolen pawn silver turned up? Had any trace been found of Joseph Musket? Had Chee heard the latest witchcraft gossip, which concerned one of the Gishi girls' seeing a big dog bothering her horses, and shooting at it with her .22, and the dog turning into a man and running away. Chee said he'd heard it. Then West switched the conversation back to Musket.

"Reckon he had anything to do with any of this?"

"With the dope business or the witch business?"

"Dope," West said. "You know he was a con. Maybe he got wind of it some way. Jailhouse telegraph. I've heard of that. Maybe he's into it. You think of that?"

"Yes," Chee said. "I've thought of that. Something else I've thought of. If you're serious about trying to find whatever it is we're looking for, I think I'd forget it. Whoever has that stuff is going to have the worst kind of trouble. If the feds don't get him, the owner will."

"You're right," West said.

Chee got up. He took the envelope out of his pocket.

"Is this really the three of diamonds in here?"

"Whatever you said it was. Three of diamonds, I think you said."

Chee opened the envelope. He pulled out the three of diamonds.

"How do you do that?"

"Magic," West said, grinning.

"I can't figure out the angle."

West spread his great hands. "I'm a magician," he said. "For years, a professional. With the circus in the good days and then many years with the carnivals."

"But you're not going to tell me how it works?"

"Takes the fun out of it," West said. "Just think about it as mind over matter."

"Thanks for the coffee," Chee said. He put on his hat. "Fine-looking boy you've got there." Chee nodded toward the photographs. "Is he still in the Marines?"

All the easy mobility left West's big face. It froze. "He was killed," he said.

"I'm sorry," Chee said. "In the Marines?"

He wished he hadn't asked the question. West wasn't going to answer it. But he did.

"After he got out," West said. "He made some bad friends in El Paso. They killed him."

7

◆

At dawn, Chee parked the pickup at the windmill. He slammed the door behind him and stood facing the glow on the eastern horizon. He yawned and stretched and inhaled deeply of the cold early air. He felt absolutely fine. This was *hozro*. This was the beauty that Changing Woman taught them to attain. This was the feeling of harmony, of being in tune. The orange glow in the east turned to a hot yellow as Chee sang his dawn chant. There was no one in miles to hear him. He shouted it, greeting Dawn Boy, greeting the sun, blessing the new day. "Let beauty walk before me," Chee sang. "Let beauty walk behind me. Let beauty walk all around me." He opened his shirt, extracted his medicine pouch, took out a pinch of pollen, and offered it to the moving air. "In beauty it is finished," Chee sang.

The mood continued through breakfast—hot coffee from his stainless-steel thermos and two sandwiches of bologna and thin, hard Hopi *piki* bread. As he chewed he reviewed. Did Joseph Musket disappear to set up a narcotics hijacking? Was the burglary done simply to provide a cover motive for his disappearance? That would explain why none of the missing jewelry had turned up. Or had Joseph Musket's disappearance some connection with the murder of John Doe? The burglary had been two nights after they'd brought in Doe's body. Could Musket have intentionally provoked West into firing him because—once the body was found—there

39

was some reason he had to run and he wanted to run without causing suspicion? For a moment that seemed to make some sense. But only for a moment. Then Chee remembered that there hadn't been any genuine effort to hide the body. It had been left along the path to Kisigi Spring. Isolated and not often used, but the only route to an important Hopi shrine, if Dashee knew what he was talking about. That provoked another thought. If you could learn from the Hopis when the shrine was visited, you could get a closer estimation—or maybe you could—of when the man had been killed there. All they had now was the medical examiner's casual estimate of "dead not more than a month, not less than two weeks." Would knowing when the body appeared on the trail help?

Chee took another bite, chewed, and thought about it. He couldn't see how. But who knows? At the moment he felt supremely optimistic. A brace of horned larks were singing their morning song beyond the windmill and the air was cool against his face and the crusty *piki* bread was tasting of wheat and bacon fat in his mouth. Someday he would unravel John Doe. Someday he would find Joseph Musket. (Why do they call you Ironfingers?) Someday, perhaps even today, he would catch the man who was vandalizing this windmill. He felt in harmony with all such things this morning—capable even of persuading these strange Black Mesa Navajos to confide in him about their witch. In a moment the sun would be high enough to give him the slanting light he needed to read even the faintest tracks. Then he would see what he could learn about this latest vandalism. Probably he would learn nothing very much. But even if the hard-packed, drought-baked earth told him nothing at all, that, too, would be right and proper, in tune with his relationship with this ugly windmill and the vandal who so hated it. Sooner or later he would understand this business. He'd find the cause. Senseless as it seemed, there'd be a reason behind it. The wind did not move, the leaf did not fall, the bird did not cry, nor did the windmill provoke such violent anger without a reason. All was part of the universal pattern, as Changing Woman had taught them when she formed the first four Navajo clans. Jim Chee had ingested that fact with his mother's milk, and from the endless lessons his uncle taught him. "All is order," Hosteen Nakai taught him. "Look for the pattern."

Chee left half the coffee in the thermos and wrapped a towel around the bottle. That, with two more bologna sandwiches still in his sack, would serve for lunch. A covey of Gambel's quail, their long topknot feathers bobbing, paraded single file along the slope below the windmill, heading for the arroyo a hundred yards to the north. The quail would be after an early-morning drink. Far down the arroyo three cottonwoods stood—two alive and one a long-dead skeleton. They were the only such trees in miles and must mark a shallow water table. Perhaps a spring. Without some source of water, the drought would force all birds away from here.

Chee found scuff marks on the earth, left by the vandal and by the Hopi who had discovered the vandalism. They told him nothing useful. Then he examined the mill itself. This time the vandal had used some sort of lever to kink the long connecting rod that tied the gear mechanism overhead to the pump cylinder in the well casing. It was an efficient means of destruction which left the force of the turning blades and the pumping action to strip the gears. But the vandal was exhausting such opportunities. Now the footing bolts were securely brazed into place, and the gearbox was secured. The custodians of the windmill could easily prevent a repetition of this new outrage by using a two-inch pipe to provide a protective sleeve for the pump rod. Chee scrutinized the mill thoughtfully, looking for weak points. He found nothing that could be damaged without some sort of special equipment. A portable cutting torch,

41

for example, could take a slice out of one of the metal legs and topple the whole affair again, or make hash out of the gearbox once more. But the vandal so far hadn't used anything sophisticated. Horses, a rope, a steel bar—nothing complicated. What could a man without equipment do now to cause serious damage? The best he could find involved putting the mill in neutral to stop pump action, then pouring cement down the pump shaft. That would require only a small plastic funnel, a sack of cement, some sand, and a bucket. Maybe a ten-dollar investment. And the solution would be permanent.

The sun was higher now and Chee broadened his search, covering the ground in widening circles. He found hoofprints and human tracks, but nothing interesting. Then he dropped into the arroyo and scouted it—first upstream and then down. Someone who wore moccasins had used its sandy bottom often as a pathway. The moccasins were surprising. Navajos—even old people—almost never wore them, and as far as Chee knew, Hopis used them only when ceremonial occasions demanded.

The path ended at the cottonwoods. As Chee had guessed, there was water seepage here in wetter seasons and the moisture had produced a robust growth of tamarisk bushes, chamiso, Russian olives, and assorted arid country weeds. The path disappeared into this cover and Chee followed it. He found the origin of the seep. Here the arroyo had cut its way past an outcropping of hard gray shale. Seeping water had eaten away at this formation, leaving a cavity perhaps four feet high, three times as wide, and as deep as Chee's vision would go into the shaded darkness. The rock here was stained green with now-dead algae and covered with a heavy growth of lichen. Chee squatted, studying the shale. The morning breeze moved through the brush around him, died away, and rose again. Chee's eye caught movement back in the shadowy cavity. He saw a feather flutter and two tiny yellow eyes.

"Ah," Chee said. He moved forward on hands and knees. The eyes were painted on a stick—a tiny semi-face framed by two downy feathers. Behind this stick in an irregular row were others, scores of them—a little forest of feathered plumes.

Chee touched nothing. He perched on hands and knees and studied the shrine and the prayer plumes which decorated it. The Hopis called them *pahos*, he remembered, and offered them as gifts to the spirits. Those that Chee could see well from his position seemed to have been made by one man. The carved shapes were similar and the mix of colors was the same. One, he noticed, had toppled. Chee examined it. One of the feathers was bent but the paint was fresh. It seemed to be the newest of the *pahos*. An unhappy kachina rejecting this season's gift? Or had some clumsy intruder knocked the *paho* over?

Back at his pickup at noon, Chee fished his lunch out of the glove box. He sat with his feet out the open door and ate slowly, sorting the odds and ends of information he had accumulated during the morning. Nothing much. But not a total waste. The spring, for example, provided a good view of the windmill. Whoever tended it might have seen the vandal. He washed down the sandwich with a sip of coffee. How had West done the card trick? Name a card. Chee had named the three of diamonds. West had handed him the three sealed in a little envelope. There seemed no way it could be done. He went over it again, in his memory. He'd said, "Three of diamonds," and West's hand had dipped into the left-hand pocket of his coveralls and extracted the envelope. What would West have done if Chee had said jack of clubs? He thought about it. Then he chuckled. He knew how the trick was done. He glanced at his watch. A little after noon. A flock of red-winged blackbirds had been foraging along the arroyo. They moved from one growth of Russian olive toward another, veered suddenly, and settled in another growth, farther up the arroyo. Chee was chewing the first bite of his second sandwich. His jaws stopped. His eyes examined the area. They saw nothing. The chewing began again. Chee finished the sandwich, drained the thermos. A dove flew down the gully. It banked abruptly away from the same growth of olives. Chee drank. The only thing that would arouse such caution in birds would be a human. Someone was watching him. Was there a way he could approach the olive brush without alerting the watcher? Chee could see none.

He put the thermos on the seat. Who would the watcher be? Perhaps Johnson, or one of Johnson's people from the DEA, hoping Chee would lead them to the stolen stuff. Perhaps the windmill vandal. Perhaps the Hopi who tended the shrine. Or perhaps God knows who. The air was almost motionless here, but a swirl of breeze started a dust devil across Wepo Wash. It moved into the wash, and across it, coming obliquely toward Chee. Over his head, the windmill groaned as its blades began turning. But the pump rod was motionless. The gearing mechanism which connected the rod to the fan was gone now—away to have its vandalism repaired—and the mill pumped nothing. Chee tried again to calculate who the vandal might be. Not enough information. He tried again to calculate who might abe watching him. No luck. He reexamined his solution to the card trick and found it correct. Why had the pilot flown into the rocks? Chee locked the truck and began walking toward Wepo Wash.

He walked parallel to the arroyo, watching the blackbirds. If the birds were startled out of the olive grove where they were now feeding, it would signal that his watcher was following him—moving down the arroyo toward the wash. If not, he'd guess the watcher was more interested in the windmill than in a Navajo cop. The birds rose with a clatter of sound and flew back up the arroyo to the trees they had been avoiding. Chee had expected them to do exactly that.

8

◆

The only reasons Jimmy Chee would have admitted for climbing down into Wepo Wash was to give himself a chance to identify—and perhaps even confront—whoever was watching him. He'd give the watcher time to follow. Then he would drop out of sight—probably by moving into a side arroyo somewhere up the wash. Once Chee was out of sight, the watcher would have to make a decision: to follow or not. However he made it, Chee would be able to reverse the roles. He'd become the stalker.

That was the plan. But now he was in the wash, and just a hundred yards up the hard-packed sandy bottom from where he stood, the sun glinted from the remains of the aircraft. The wreckage was FBI and DEA business. A Navajo Tribal Policeman would not be welcome here without a specific invitation. But Chee was curious. And to his watcher, a visit to the wreckage would seem a logical reason for this walk.

The ground around the site was thoroughly trampled now and the plane itself had been ransacked. Wing and stabilizer panels had been peeled open, a gas tank removed, and holes punched in the thin aluminum skin of the rudder, in what must have been a search for the cargo it had carried. Chee stared up the wash, up the plane's landing path, frowning. As he remembered, it had struck an upthrust of basalt which jutted from the floor of the wash. The wash had flowed

46

around the extrusion on both sides, eroding the earth and leaving a black stone island in a sea of sand. If there wasn't room to land upwash from this wall of stone, and there seemed to be plenty of space, there was obviously room enough to miss it to the right or left. Why hadn't the pilot avoided it? Surely he hadn't simply landed blindly in the dark. Chee walked upwash, out of the trampled area. He kept his eyes on the sand, looking for the answer. The watcher could wait.

A little more than an hour later, he heard the sound of a car engine. By then he knew why the plane had crashed. But he had new questions.

The car was a dark-blue Ford Bronco. It pulled to a stop beside the wreckage. Two persons emerged. A man and a woman. They stood a moment, looking upwash toward Chee, and then walked to the aircraft. Chee walked toward them. The man was tall, hatless, gray-haired, wearing jeans and a white shirt. The woman was hatless, too. She was rather small, with short dark hair that curled around her face. Not FBI. Probably not DEA, although anybody could be DEA. They stood beside the wreckage, looking at the plane but waiting for him. Chee saw the man was older than he had looked from a distance—perhaps in his early fifties. One of those men who take care of themselves, join racquet clubs, jog, lift weights. His face was long, with deep lines along the nose, and eyes which, because of large black pupils, looked somewhat moist and luminous. The woman glanced at Chee and then stared at the wreckage. Her oval face, drained of color, looked shocked. She was in her fifties, Chee guessed, but at the moment she looked as old as time. Something about her tugged at Chee's memory. The man's expression was defensive, the look of someone caught trespassing, who expects to be asked who he is and what he's doing. Chee nodded to him.

"We came out to see the aircraft," the man said. "I

was his attorney and this is Gail Pauling."

"Jim Chee," Chee said. He shook the man's hand and nodded to the woman.

"Jim Chee," the woman said. "You're the one who found my brother."

Chee knew now what she reminded him of. Her brother was the pilot. "I don't think he had any suffering," Chee said. "It must have happened in an instant. Too quick to know what happened."

"And what did happen?" Miss Pauling asked. She gestured toward the outcrop. "I can't believe he would just fly right into this."

"He didn't, exactly," Chee said. "His wheels touched down about fifty yards up there. He was on the ground."

She was staring at the wreckage, her face still stunned. Chee wasn't sure she had heard him. "Something must have happened to him," she said, as if to herself. "He would never have flown right into this."

"It was in the dark," Chee said. "Didn't they tell you that?"

"They didn't tell me anything," Miss Pauling said. She seemed to really see Chee for the first time. "Just that he crashed, and he was dead, and the police think he was flying in some contraband, and that a policeman named Jim Chee was the one who saw it all."

"I didn't see it," Chee said. "I heard it. It was a couple of hours before dawn. The moon was down." Chee described what had happened. The lawyer listened intently, his moist eyes studying Chee's face. Chee didn't mention hearing the shot, or the other sounds.

The woman's face was incredulous. "He landed in the pitch dark?" she asked. "He used to be in the Tactical Air Force. But on an airfield. And with radar. I worried about it. But I can't believe he'd just land blind."

"He didn't," Chee said. He gestured up the bed of the wash. "He'd landed at least three times before. Just a day or two earlier, the way the tracks look. Probably in the day-light. Practicing, I'd guess. And then when he made this landing, he had lights."

"Lights?" the lawyer asked.

"It looks like battery lanterns," Chee said. "A row of them on the ground."

Miss Pauling was staring up the wash, looking baffled.

"They left their marks," Chee explained. "I'll show you."

He led them down the side of the wash. Was the watcher still out there somewhere? If he was, what would he think of all this? If the watcher was Johnson, or one of Johnson's DEA people assigned to follow Chee, he'd never believe this meeting was not prearranged. Chee considered that. It didn't bother him.

They walked along the narrow strip of shade cast by the almost vertical wall of the wash. Beyond this shadow, the sunlight glittered from the gray-yellow surface of the arroyo bottom. Heat waves shimmered from the flatness and the only sound was boot soles on the sand.

Behind him the lawyer cleared his throat. "Mr. Chee," he said. "That car you mentioned in your report, driving away—did you get a look at it?"

"You read the report?" Chee asked. He was surprised, but he didn't look around. It was exactly what Largo had predicted.

"We stopped at your police station at Tuba City," the attorney said. "They showed it to me."

Of course, Chee thought. Why not? The man was the attorney of the accident victim. The attorney and the next of kin.

"It was gone," Chee said. "I heard the engine starting. A car or maybe a pickup truck."

"The shot," the attorney asked. "Rifle? Shotgun? Pistol?"

That's an interesting question, Chee thought. "Not a shot-gun. Probably a pistol," he said. The memory of the sound

49

echoed in his mind. Probably a large pistol.

"Would you say a twenty-two, or something larger? A thirty-two? A thirty-eight?"

Another interesting question. "I'd be guessing," Chee said.

"Would you mind?"

"I'd guess a thirty-eight, or larger," Chee said. What would the next question be? Chee's guess at who pulled the trigger, maybe.

"I've always been interested in guns," the lawyer said.

And then they were opposite the place where the plane had first touched down. Chee moved out of the shade and walked into the glittering heat. He squatted beside the marks.

"Here," he said. "See? Here's where the right wheel first touched." He pointed. "And there the left wheel. He had the plane almost exactly level."

Near this touchdown point, a line about two inches deep had been drawn across the sand. Chee rose and took a dozen steps down the track. "Here the nose wheel touched," he said. "I think Pauling drew that line to mark the place. And over there . . . See the tracks?" Chee pointed toward the center of the wash. "That's where he took off both times."

"Or maybe he landed over there and took off here," the lawyer said in his soft voice. He laughed a mild, soft sound. "But what difference is it?"

"Not much," Chee said. "But he did land here. Deeper impression at the impact point, and the bounce marks. And if you go over there and take a close look, you notice the sand is blown back more on the tracks where he lifted off. Engine really revving up then, you know, and idling when he landed."

The attorney's soft eyes were examining Chee. "Yes," he said. "Of course. Can you still read that in the sand?"

"If you look," Chee said.

Miss Pauling was staring down the wash toward the wreckage. "But if he touched down here, he had plenty of time to stop. He had more room than he needed."

"The night he crashed, he didn't touch down here," Chee said. He walked toward the wreckage. A hundred yards, two hundred yards. Finally he stopped. He squatted again, touched a faint indentation in the sand with a fingertip. "Here was the first lantern," he said. He glanced over his shoulder. "And his wheels touched right there. See? Just a few feet past the lantern."

Miss Pauling looked at the wheel tracks and then past them at the wreckage, looming just ahead of them. "My God," she said. "He didn't have a chance, did he?"

"Somebody put out five lanterns in a straight line between here and the rock." Chee pointed. "There were five more lanterns on the other side of the rock."

The lawyer was staring at Chee, lips slightly parted. He read the implications of the lantern placement instantly. Miss Pauling was thinking of something else. "Did he have his landing lights on? Your report didn't mention that."

"I didn't see any light," Chee said. "I think I would have seen the glow."

"So he was depending on whoever put the lanterns out," Miss Pauling said. Then what Chee had said about the lanterns beyond the rock finally reached her. She looked at him, her face startled. "Five more lanterns beyond the rock? Behind it?"

"Yes," Chee said. He felt a pity for the woman. To lose your brother is bad. To learn someone killed him is worse.

"But why . . . ?"

Chee shook his head. "Maybe somebody wanted him to land but not to take off," he said. "I don't know. Maybe I'm wrong about the lanterns. All I found was the little depressions. Like this one."

She stared at him wordlessly. Studying him. "You don't think you're wrong."

"Well, no," Chee said. "This little oval shape, with these sharp indentations around the edge—it looks just the size and shape for those dry-cell batteries you attach the lantern bulb to. I'll measure it and check, but I don't know what else it would be."

"No," Miss Pauling said. She released a long breath, and with it her shoulders slumped. A little life seemed to leave her. "I don't know what else it would be, either." Miss Pauling's face had changed. It had hardened. "Somebody killed him."

"These lanterns," the lawyer said. "They were gone when you got here? They weren't mentioned in your report."

"They were gone," Chee said. "I found the trace of them just before you drove up. When I was here before, it was dark."

"But they weren't in the follow-up report either. The one that was made after the airplane was searched and all that. That was done in the daytime."

"That was federal cops," Chee said. "I guess they didn't notice the marks."

The lawyer looked at Chee thoughtfully. "I wouldn't have," he said finally. He smiled. "I've always heard that Indians were good trackers."

A long time ago, in his senior year at the University of New Mexico, Chee had resolved never to let such generalizations irritate him. It was a resolution he rarely managed to keep.

"I am a Navajo," Chee said. "We don't have a word in our language for 'Indians.' Just specific words. For Utes, and Hopis, and Apaches. A white is a *belacani*, a Mexican is a *nakai*. So forth. Some Navajos are good at tracking. Some aren't. You learn it by studying it. Like law."

"Of course," the lawyer said. He was still observing Chee. "But how do you learn it?"

"I had a teacher," Chee said. "My mother's brother. He

showed me what to look for." Chee stopped. He was not in the mood to discuss tracking with this odd stranger.

"Like what?" the lawyer said.

Chee tried to think of examples. He shrugged. "You see a man walk by. You go look at the tracks he made. You see him walk by, carrying something heavy in one hand. You look at the tracks. You go again tomorrow to look at the tracks after a day. And after two days. You see a fat man and a thin man squatting in the shade, talking. When they leave, you go and look at the marks a fat man makes when he squats on his heels, and the marks a thin man makes." Chee stopped again. He was thinking of his uncle, in the Chuska high country tracking the mule deer. Showing how the bucks dragged their hooves when rutting, how to estimate the age of a doe by reading the splaying of its cloven toes in its tracks. Of his uncle kneeling beside the track left in the drying mud by a pickup truck, testing the moisture in a ridge of dirt, showing him how to estimate how many hours had passed since the tire had left that print. Much more than that, of course. But he had said enough to satisfy courtesy.

The lawyer had taken out his billfold. He extracted a business card and handed it to Chee.

"I'm Ben Gaines," he said. "I'll be representing Mr. Pauling's estate. Could I hire you? In your spare time?"

"For what?"

"For pretty much what you'd do anyway." Ben Gaines gestured toward the wreck. "Putting together just exactly what happened here."

"I won't be doing that," Chee said. "This isn't my case. This is a first-degree felony. It involves non-Navajos. This was part of the Navajo-Hopi Joint Use Reservation, but now it's Hopi. Outside my territory. Outside my jurisdiction. I'm here working on something else. Came down here because I was curious."

"All the better," Gaines said. "There won't be any question of conflict of interest."

"I'm not sure the rules would allow it," Chee said. "I'd have to check with the captain." It occured to Chee that one way or another he'd be doing what the lawyer wanted. His curiosity would demand it.

Gaines was chuckling. "I was just thinking that it might be just as well if your boss didn't know about this arrangement. Nothing wrong with it. But if you ask a bureaucrat if there's a rule against something, he'll always tell you there is."

"Yeah," Chee said. "What do you want me to do?"

"I want to know what happened to Pauling here," Gaines said. "The report sounded like there were three people here when it happened. I want to know for sure. You heard a shot. Then you heard a car, or maybe a truck, driving away. I want to know what went on." Gaines waved around him. "Maybe you can find some tracks that'll tell."

"Plenty of tracks now," Chee said. "About a dozen federal cops, Arizona State Police, county law, so forth, trampling all around. And yours and mine and hers." Chee nodded to Miss Pauling. She had walked back to the wreckage and stood staring at the cabin.

"My law firm pays forty dollars an hour for work like this," Gaines said. "Find out what you can."

"I'll let you know," Chee said, making the answer deliberately ambiguous. "What else you want to know?"

"I get the impression," Gaines said slowly, "that the police aren't sure what happened to the car you heard driving away. They don't seem to think it ever left this part of the country. I'd like to know what you can find out about that."

"Find out what happened to the car?"

"If you can," Gaines said.

"It would help if I knew what I was looking for," Chee said.

54

Gaines hesitated a long moment. "Yes," he said. "It would. Just tell me what you find out."

"Where?"

"We'll be staying at that motel the Hopis run. Up on Second Mesa," Gaines said.

Chee nodded.

Gaines hesitated again. "One other thing," he said. "I've heard there was a cargo on that plane. If you happened to turn that up, there'd be a reward for that. I'm sure some pay-out would be available from the owners if that turned up." Gaines smiled at Chee, his eyes friendly and moist. "A big one. If you happen onto that, let me know about it. Quietly. Then I'll get to work and find out a way to get into contact with whoever owned whatever it was. You find the stuff. I find the owners. Sort of a partnership between the two of us. You know what I mean?"

"Yes," Chee said. "I know."

9

The late-afternoon sun slanted through the windows of the Burnt Water Trading Post, breaking the cavernous interior into a patchwork of harsh contrasts. Dazzling reflected sunlight alternated with cool darkness. And in the sunlight, dust motes danced. They reminded Chee of drought.

"Shrine?" Jake West said. "Hell, between you people and the Hopi, this country is covered up with shrines." West was sitting in a patch of darkness, his heavy bearded head silhouetted against an oblong of sunlight on the wall.

"This one is in the arroyo just east of the windmill," Chee said. "By a dried-up spring. It's full of prayer plumes. Some of 'em fresh, so somebody's been taking care of it."

"*Pahos,*" West said. "You call 'em prayer plumes, but for the Hopis they're *pahos.*"

"Whatever," Chee said. "You know anything about it?"

Through the open front door came the sound of a car, moving fast, jolting into the trading post yard. Over the noise, West said he didn't know anything about the shrine. "Never heard of that one" he said. There was the sound of a car door slamming. The smell of aroused dust drifted to their nostrils.

"That Cowboy?" Chee asked.

"Hope so," West said. "Hope there's not somebody else that parks like that. You'd think they'd teach the sons-a-bitches how to park without raising a cloud of dust. Ought to teach that before they let 'em into a car."

At the door a bulky young man in a khaki uniform paused to exchange remarks with a cluster of old men passing the afternoon in the shade. Whatever he said provoked an elderly chuckle.

"Come on in, Cowboy," West said. "Chee here needs some information."

"As usual," Cowboy said. He grinned at Chee. "You caught your windmill vandal yet?"

"Our windmill vandal," Chee corrected. "You solved the great airplane mystery?"

"Not quite," Cowboy said. "But progress has been made." He extracted an eight-by-ten glossy photograph from a folder he was carrying and displayed it. "Here's the dude we're looking for. You guys see him, promptly inform either Deputy Sheriff Albert Dashee or call your friendly Coconino County Sheriff's Department."

"Who is he?" West said. The photograph obviously had been blown up from a standard police mug identification shot. It showed a man in his middle forties, with gray hair, close-set eyes, and a high, narrow forehead dominating a long, narrow face.

"Name's Richard Palanzer, also known as Dick Palanzer. What the feds call a 'known associate of the narcotics traffic.' All they told me is he was indicted a couple of years ago in Los Angeles County for conspiracy, narcotics. They want us looking for him around here."

"Where'd the picture come from?" Chee asked. He turned it over and looked at the back, which turned out to be bare.

"Sheriff," Cowboy said. "He got it from the DEA people. This is the bird they think drove off with the dope after the plane crash." Cowboy accepted the photograph back from Chee. "That is if Chee didn't do the driving. I understand the feds can't decide whether Chee rode shotgun or drove."

West looked puzzled. He raised his eyebrows, looked from Dashee to Chee and back.

Dashee laughed. "Just a joke," he said. "Chee was out there when it happened, so the DEA was suspicious. They're suspicious of everybody. Including me, and you, and that fellow over there." Dashee indicated a geriatric Hopi who was easing himself out of the front door with the help of an aluminum walker and a solicitous middle-aged woman. "What was it Chee wanted to know?"

"There's a little shrine in that arroyo by the windmill," Chee said. "By a dried-up spring. Lots of *pahos* in it. Looks like somebody's taking care of it. You know anything about it?"

At the word "shrine," Cowboy's expression changed from joviality to neutrality. Cowboy was listed on the payroll of the Coconino County, Arizona, Sheriff's Department as Albert Dashee, Jr. He'd accumulated sixty hours credit at Northern Arizona University before saying to hell with it. But he was Angushtiyo, or "Crow Boy," to his family, a member of the Side Corn Clan, and a valuable man in the Kachina Society of his village of Shipaulovi. Chee was becoming a friend, but Crow Boy was Hopi and Chee Navajo, and shrines, any shrines, involved the Hopi religion.

"What do you want to know?" Cowboy asked.

"From where it is, you can see the windmill," Chee said. "Whoever tends it might have seen something." He shrugged. "Long shot. But I've got nothing else."

"The *pahos*," Cowboy said. "Some of them new? Like somebody is taking care of it now?"

"I didn't look at them real close," Chee said. "I didn't want to touch anything." He wanted Cowboy to know that. "But I'd say some were old and some were new and somebody is taking care of it."

Cowboy thought. "It wouldn't be one of ours. I mean not Shipaulovi village. That's not our village land. I think that land down there belongs either to Walpi or to one of the kiva societies. I'll have to see what I can find out."

As the Navajos saw it, the land down there was Navajo land, allotted to the family of Patricia Gishi. But this wasn't the time for renewing the old Joint Use arguments.

"Just a long shot," Chee said. "But who knows?"

"I'll ask around," Cowboy repeated. "Did you know they're fixing that windmill again today?" He grinned. "You ready for that?"

Chee was not ready for that. It depressed him. The windmill would be vandalized again—as certain as fate. Chee knew it in his bones, and he knew there was nothing he could do to stop it from happening. Not until he understood what was happening. When the new vandalism happened it would be Cowboy's fault as much as his own, but Cowboy didn't seem to mind. Cowboy wouldn't have to stand in Captain Largo's office, and hear Captain Largo reading the indignant memo from the pertinent bureaucrat in the Bureau of Indian Affairs, and have Largo's mild eyes examining him, with the unspoken question in them relative to his competence to keep a windmill safe.

"With the BIA doing it, I thought it would be Christmas before they got it done," Chee said. "What the hell happened?"

"Something must have gone wrong," West said.

"The BIA got efficient. It happens every eight or ten years," Cowboy said. "Anyway, I saw a truck going in there. They said they had all the parts and they was fixing it today."

"I think you can relax," West said. "They probably got the wrong parts."

"You going to stake it out again?" Cowboy asked.

"I don't think that will work now," Chee said. "The plane crash screwed that up. Whoever it was learned I was out there. They'll make damn sure next time nobody's watching."

"The vandal was out there the night the plane crashed?" West asked.

"Somebody was," Chee said. "I heard somebody climbing out of the wash. And then while I was busy with the crash, somebody screwed up the windmill again."

"I didn't know that," West said. "You mean the vandal was right down there by the wreck? After it happened?"

"That's right," Chee said. "I'm surprised everybody didn't know that by now. They're handing the report around for everybody to read." Chee told West and Cowboy about the lawyer and the sister of the pilot.

"They was in here yesterday morning, asking for directions," West said. "They wanted to find the airplane, and they wanted to find you." West was frowning. "You mean to tell me that fellow had read the police report?"

"That's not so unusual," Cowboy said. "Not if he is the lawyer for somebody involved. Lawyers do that all the time if there's something they want to know."

"So he said he was the pilot's lawyer," West said. "What was his name?"

"Gaines," Chee said.

"What did he want to know?" West asked.

"He wanted to know what happened."

"Hell," West said. "Easy enough to see what happened. Fellow ran his airplane into a rock."

Chee shrugged.

"He wanted to know more than that?" West persisted.

"He wanted to find the car. The one that drove away after the crash."

"He figured it was still out there somewhere, then?"

"Seemed to," Chee said. He wanted to change the subject. "Either one of you heard any gossip about a witch killing a man out in Black Mesa somewhere?"

Cowboy laughed. "Sure," he said. "You remember that body was picked up last July—the one that was far gone?"

60

Cowboy wrinkled his nose at the unpleasant memory.

"John Doe?" Chee asked. "A witch killed him? Where'd that come from?"

"And it was one of your Navajo witches," Dashee said. "Not one of our *powaqa*."

10

Cowboy Dashee didn't know much about why the gossipers believed John Doe had been killed by a witch. But once he got over his surprise that Chee was sincerely interested, that Chee would attach importance to such a tale, he was willing to run the rumor to earth. They took Dashee's patrol car up Third Mesa to Bacobi. There Cowboy talked to the man who had passed the tale along to him. The man sent them over to Second Mesa to see a woman at Mishongovi. Dashee spent a long fifteen minutes in her house and came out smiling.

"Struck gold," Cowboy said. "We go to Shipaulovi."

"Find where the report started?" Chee asked.

"Better than that," Cowboy said. "We found the man who found the body."

Albert Lomatewa brought three straight-backed chairs out of the kitchen, and set them in a curved row just outside the door of his house. He invited them both to sit, and sat himself. He extracted a pack of cigarets, offered each of them a smoke, and smoked himself. The children who had been playing there (Lomatewa's great-grandchildren, Chee guessed) moved a respectful distance away and muted their raucous game. Lomatewa smoked, and listened while Deputy Sheriff Dashee talked. Dashee told him who Chee was, and that it was their job to identify the man who had been found on Black Mesa, and to find out who had shot him, and to learn everything they could about it. "There's been a lot of gossip about this man," Dashee said, speaking in English, "but we were told that if we came to Shipaulovi and talked to you about it, you would tell us the facts."

Lomatewa listened. He smoked his cigaret. He tapped the ash off on the ground beside his chair. He said, "It is true that there's nothing but gossip now. Nobody has any respect for anything anymore." Lomatewa reached behind him, his hand groped against the wall, found a walking cane which had been leaning there, and laid it across his legs. Last week he'd gone to Flagstaff with his granddaughter's husband, he told them, and visited another granddaughter there. "They all acted just like *bahanas*," Lomatewa said. "Drinking beer around the house. Laying in bed in the morning. Just like white people." Lomatewa's fingers played with the stick as he talked of the modernism he had found in his family at Flagstaff, but he was watching Jim Chee, watching Cowboy Dashee. Watching them skeptically. The performance, the attitude, were familiar. Chee had noticed it before, in his own paternal grandfather and in others. It had nothing to do with a Hopi talking of sensitive matters in front of a Navajo. It involved being on the downslope of your years, disappointed, and a little bitter. Lomatewa obviously knew who Cowboy was. Chee knew the deputy well enough to doubt he was a solidly orthodox Hopi. Lomatewa's statement had drifted into a complaint against the Hopi Tribal Council.

"We weren't told to do it that way," Lomatewa said. "The way it was supposed to be, the villages did their own business. The *kikmongwi*, and the societies, and the kiva. There wasn't any tribal council. That's a *bahana* idea."

Chee allowed the pause to stretch a respectful few moments. Cowboy leaned forward, raised a hand, opened his mouth.

Chee cut him off. "That's like what my uncle taught me," Chee said. "He said we must always respect the old ways. That we must stay with them."

Lomatewa looked at him. He smiled his skeptical smile. "You're a policeman for the *bahanas*," he said. "Have you listened to your uncle?"

"I am a policeman for my own people," Chee said. "And I am studying with my uncle to be a *yataalii*." He saw the Navajo word meant nothing to Lomatewa. "I am studying to be a singer, a medicine man. I know the Blessing Way, and the Night Chant, and someday I will know some of the other ceremonials."

Lomatewa examined Chee, and Cowboy Dashee, and Chee again. He took the cane in his right hand and made a mark with its tip in the dust. "This place is the spruce shrine," he said. He glanced at Cowboy. "Do you know where that is?"

"It is Kisigi Spring, Grandfather," said Cowboy, passing the test.

Lomatewa nodded. He drew a crooked line in the dust. "We came down from the spring at the dawn," he said. "Everything was right. But about midmorning we saw this boot standing there in the path. This boy who was with us said somebody had lost a boot, but you could see it wasn't that. If the boot had just fallen there, it would fall over on its side." He looked at Chee for agreement. Chee nodded.

Lomatewa shrugged. "Behind the boot was the body of the Navajo." He pursed his lips and shrugged again. The recitation was ended.

"What day was that, Grandfather?" Chee asked.

"It was the fourth day before the Niman Kachina," Lomatewa said.

"This Navajo," Chee said. "When we got the body, there wasn't much left. But the doctors said it was a man about thirty. A man who must have weighed about one hundred sixty pounds. Is that about right?"

Lomatewa thought about it. "Maybe a little older," he said. "Maybe thirty-two or so."

"Was it anyone you had seen before?" Cowboy asked.

"All Navajos—" Lomatewa began. He stopped, glanced at Chee. "I don't think so," he said.

"Grandfather," Cowboy said. "When you go for the sacred spruce, you use the same trail coming and going. That is what I have been taught. Could the body have been there under that brush the day before, when you went up to the spring?"

"No," Lomatewa said. "It wasn't there. The witch put it there during the night."

"Witch?" Cowboy Dashee asked. "Would it have been a Hopi *powaqa* or a Navajo witch?"

Lomatewa looked at Chee, frowning. "You said that you and this Navajo policeman got the body. Didn't he see what had been done?"

"When we got the body, Grandfather, the ravens had been there for days, and the coyotes, and the vultures," Cowboy said. "You could only tell it had been a man and that he had been dead a long time in the heat."

"Ah," Lomatewa said. "Well, his hands had been skinned." Lomatewa threw out his hands, palms up, demonstrating. "Fingers, palms, all. And the bottoms of his feet." He noticed Cowboy's puzzled surprise and nodded toward Chee. "If this Navajo respects his people's old ways, he will understand."

Chee understood, perfectly. "That's what the witch uses to make corpse powder," Chee explained to Cowboy. "They call it *anti'l*. You make it out of the skin that has the individual's soul stamped into it." Chee pointed to the fingerprint whorls on his fingertips and the pads of his hands. "Like on your palms, and fingers, and the soles of your feet, and the glans of your penis." As he explained, it occurred to Jim Chee that he could finally answer one of Captain Largo's questions. There was more than the usual witchcraft gossip on Black Mesa because there was a witch at work.

11

By the time Chee drove back to Tuba City, typed up his report, and left it on Captain Largo's desk, it was after 9:00 P.M. By the time he let himself into his trailer house and lowered himself on the edge of his bunk, he felt totally used up. He yawned, scrubbed his forearm against his face, and slumped, elbows on knees, reviewing the day and waiting for the energy to get himself ready for bed. He had tomorrow off, and the day after. He would to to Two Gray Hills, to the country of his relatives in the Chuska Mountains, far from the world of police, and narcotics, and murder. He would heat rocks and take a sweat bath with his uncle, and get back to the job of mastering the sand paintings for the Night Chant. Chee yawned again and bent to untie his boot laces, and found himself thinking of John Doe's hands as the old Hopi had described them. Bloody. Flayed. In his own mind the only memory he could recall was of bones, sinew, and bits of muscle ends which had resisted decay and the scavengers. Something about what the Hopi had said bothered him. He thought about it and couldn't place the incongruity, and yawned again, and removed his boots. John Doe had died on the fourth day before the Niman Kachina, and this year the ceremonial had been held on July 14. He'd confirmed that with Dashee. So John Doe's body had been dumped onto the path on July 10. Chee lay back on the bunk, reached out, and fished the Navajo-

Hopi telephone book off the table. It was a thin book, much bent from being carried in Chee's hip pocket, and it contained all telephone numbers in a territory a little larger than New England. Chee found the Burnt Water Trading Post listed along with a dozen or so telephones on Second Mesa. He pushed himself up on one elbow and dialed it. It rang twice.

"Hello."

"Is Jake West there?"

"This is West."

"Jim Chee," Chee said. "How good is your memory?"

"Fair."

"Any chance you remembering if Musket was at work last July eleventh? That would have been four days before the Home Dances up on Second Mesa."

"July eleventh," West said. "What's up?"

"Probably nothing," Chee said. "Just running down dead ends on your burglary."

"Just a minute. I don't remember, but I'll have it written down in my payroll book."

Chee waited. He yawned again. This was wasting his time. He unbuckled his belt and slid out of his uniform pants and tossed them to the foot of the bed. He unbuttoned his shirt. Then West was back on the line.

"July eleventh. Let's see. He didn't show up for work July tenth or the eleventh. He showed up on the twelfth."

Chee felt slightly less sleepy.

"Okay," he said. "Thanks."

"That mean anything?"

"Probably not," Chee said.

It meant, he thought after he had removed the shirt and pulled the sheet over him, that Musket might have been the man who killed John Doe. It didn't mean he was the one—only that the possibility existed. Drowsily, Chee considered it. Musket possibly was a witch. The killing of John

68

Doe possibly was the reason Musket had departed from the Burnt Water Trading Post. But Chee was too exhausted to pursue such a demanding exercise. He thought instead of Frank Sam Nakai, who was his maternal uncle and the most respected singer along the New Mexico–Arizona border. And thinking of this great shaman, this wise and kindly man, Jim Chee fell asleep.

When he awakened, there was Johnson standing beside his bunk, looking down at him.

"Time to wake up," Johnson said.

Chee sat up. Behind Johnson another man was standing, his back to Chee, sorting through the things Chee kept stored in one of the trailer's overhead compartments. The light of the rising sun was streaming through the open door.

"What the hell?" Chee said. "What are you doing to my trailer?"

"Some checking," Johnson said.

"Nothing here either," the man said.

"This is Officer Larry Collins," Johnson said, still looking at Chee. "He's my partner on this case." Officer Collins turned and looked at Chee. He grinned. He was perhaps twenty-five. Big. Unkempt blond hair dangled from under a dirty cowboy hat. His face was a mass of freckles, his eyes reckless. "Howdy," he said. "If you got any dope hidden around here, I haven't come up with it. Not yet."

Chee couldn't think of anything to say. Disbelief mixed with anger. This was incredible. He reached for his shirt, put it on, stood up in his shorts.

"Get the hell out of here," he said to Johnson.

"Not yet," Johnson said. "We're here on business."

"We'll do any business we have over at the office," Chee said. "Get out."

Collins was behind him now and it happened too quickly for Chee to ever know exactly how he did it. He found himself face down on the bunk, with his wrists twisted high behind his shoulders. He felt Johnson's hand pinning him while Collins snapped handcuffs on his wrists. It must have been something the two of them practiced, Chee thought.

They released him. Chee sat up on the bunk. His hands were cuffed behind him.

"We need to get something straight," Johnson said. "I'm the cop and you're the suspect. That Indian badge don't mean a damn thing to me."

Chee said nothing.

"Keep on looking," Johnson said to Collins. "It's got to be bulky and there can't be many places it could hide in here. Make sure you don't miss any of them."

"I haven't," Collins said. But he moved into the kitchen area and began opening drawers.

"You had a little meeting yesterday with Gaines," Johnson said. "I want to know all about that."

"Go screw yourself," Chee said.

"You and Gaines arranged a little deal, I guess. He told you what they'd be willing to pay to buy their coke back. And he told you what would happen to you if you didn't cough it up. That about right?"

Chee said nothing. Collins was looking in the oven, checking under the sink. He poured a little detergent into his palm, examined it, and rinsed it off under the tap. "I already looked everyplace once," Collins said.

"Maybe we're not going to find that coke stashed here," Johnson said. "Maybe we're not going to find the money here either. It don't look like you were that stupid. But by God you're going to tell me where to find it."

Johnson struck Chee across the face, a stinging, backhanded blow.

"The best way to do it would be unofficial," Johnson said. "You just tell me right now, and I forget where I heard it, and you can just go on being a Navajo cop. No going to jail. No nothing. We do a lot of unofficial business." He

70

grinned at Chee, a wolfish show of big, even white teeth in a sunburned red face. "Get more work done that way."

Chee's nose hurt. He felt a trickle of blood start from it, moving down his lip. His face stung and his eyes were watering. But the real effect of the blow was psychological. His mind seemed detached from all this, working at several levels. At one, it was trying to remember the last time anyone had struck him. He had been a boy when that happened, fighting with a cousin. At another level his intelligence considered what he should do, what he should say, why this was happening. And at still another, he felt simple animal rage—an instinct to kill.

He and Johnson stared at each other, neither blinking. Collins finished in the kitchen and disappeared in the tiny bath. There was the noise of him taking something apart.

"Where is it?" Johnson asked. "The plane had the stuff on it, and the people who came to get it haven't got it. We know that. We know who took it, and we know he had to have some help, and we know you were it. Where'd you take it?"

Chee tested the handcuffs behind him, hurting his wrists. The muscles in his left shoulders were cramping where Collins had strained it. "You son of a bitch," Chee said. "You're crazy."

Johnson slapped him again. Same backhand. Same place.

"You were out there," Johnson said. "We don't know how you got onto the deal, but that doesn't matter. We just want the stuff."

Chee said nothing at all.

Johnson removed his pistol from its shoulder holster. It was a revolver with a short barrel. He jammed the barrel against Chee's forehead.

"You're going to tell me," Johnson said. He cocked the pistol. "Now."

The metal of the gun barrel pressed into the skin, hard

against the bone. "If I knew where that stuff was, I'd tell you," Chee said. He was ashamed of it, but it was the truth. Johnson seemed to read it in his face. He grunted, removed the pistol, lowered the hammer, and stuck the gun back in the holster.

"You know something," Johnson said, as if to himself. He looked around at Collins, who had stopped his hunt to watch, and then stared at Chee again, thinking. "When you know a little more, there's a smart way for you to handle it. Just see to it that I get the word. An anonymous note would do it. Or call me. That way, if you don't trust the DEA not to hammer you, you'd know we couldn't prove you tried to steal the stuff. And I couldn't turn you in for killing Jerry Jansen."

Chee had his mind working again. He remembered Jansen was the body left at the plane. But how much would Johnson tell him?

"Who's Jansen?" he asked.

Johnson laughed. "Little late to ask," he said. "He's the brother of the big man himself, the one who put this all together. And the one killed on the airplane, he was big medicine, too. Relative of the people buying the shipment."

"Pauling?"

"Pauling was nothing," Johnson said. "The taxi driver. You worry about the other one."

There was the sound of breaking glass in the shower. Collins had dropped something.

"So you see, I haven't got much time to work with you," Johnson said. He was smiling. "You've got two sets of hard people stirred up. They're going to make the connection right away and they're going to be coming after you. They're going to twist that dope out of you and if you can't deliver it, they'll just keep twisting."

Chee could think of nothing helpful to say to that.

"The only way to go is the easy way," Johnson said. "You

tell me where you and Palanzer put it. I find it. Nobody is any wiser. Any other way we handle it, you're dead. Or if you're lucky you get ten to twenty in the federal pen. And with those two people killed, you wouldn't last long in federal pen."

"I don't know where it is," Chee said. "I'm not even sure what it is."

Johnson looked at him, mildly and without comment. A smell of cologne seeped into Chee's nostrils. Collins had broken his aftershave lotion. "What did Gaines want?" Johnson said. He pulled Gaines's card out of his shirt pocket and looked at it. It had been in Chee's billfold.

"He wanted to know what happened to the car. The one I heard driving off."

"How'd he know about that?"

"He read my report. At the station. He told 'em he was the pilot's lawyer."

"Why'd he give you the card?"

"He wanted me to find the car for him. I said I'd let him know."

"Can you find it?"

"I don't see how," Chee said. "Hell, it's probably in Chicago by now, or Denver, or God knows where. Why would it stay around? From what I hear, you're circulating the picture of the guy that's supposed to be driving it. This Palanzer. Why would he stick around?"

"I'll ask the questions," Johnson said.

"But don't you think Palanzer got off with the stuff? Why else are you looking for him?"

"Maybe Palanzer got it and maybe he didn't, and maybe he had a lot of help if he did. Like a Navajo tribal cop who knows this country and knows a hole they can hide it in until things cool off some."

"But—"

"Shut up," Johnson said. "This is wasting time. I'll tell

73

you what we're going to do. We're going to wait just a little while. Give you some time to think it over. I figure you've got a day or two before the people who own that dope decide to come after you. You give some thought to what they'll do to you and then you get in touch with me and we'll deal."

"One thing," Collins said from just behind Chee. "It damn sure ain't hid in here."

"But don't wait too long," Johnson said. "You haven't got much time."

12

◆

When Captain Largo worried, his round, bland face resolved itself into a pattern of little wrinkles—something like a brown honeydew melon too long off the vine. Largo was worried now. He sat ramrod straight behind his desk, an unusual position for the captain's plump body, and listened intently to what Jim Chee was saying. What Chee was saying was angry and directly to the point, and when he finished saying it, Largo got up from his chair and walked over to the window and looked out at the sunny morning.

"They pull a gun on you?" he asked.

"Right."

"Hit you? That right?"

"Right." Chee said.

"When they took off the cuffs, they told you that if you filed a complaint, their story would be you invited them in, invited them to search, they didn't lay a hand on you. That right?"

"That's it," Chee said.

Largo looked out the window some more. Chee waited. From where he stood he could see through the glass past the captain's broad back. He could see the expanse of bunch grass, bare earth, rocks, scattered cactus, which separated the police building from the straggling row of old buildings called Tuba City. The sky had the dusty look of a droughty summer. Far across the field a cloud of blue smoke emerged from the sheet-metal garage of the Navajo Road Department—a diesel engine being test run. Largo seemed to be watching the smoke.

"Two days, they said, before the people who owned the dope figured you had it. Right?"

"That's what Johnson said," Chee agreed.

"He sound like he was guessing, or like he knew?" Largo was still looking out the window, his face away from Chee.

"Of course he was guessing," Chee said. "How would he know?"

Largo came back and sat at the desk again. He fiddled with whatever odds and ends he kept in the top drawer.

"Here's what I want you to do," he said. "Write all this down and sign it, and date it, and give it to me. Then you take some time off. You got two days coming. Take a whole week. Get the hell away from here for a while."

"Write it down? What good will that do?"

"Good to have it," Largo said. "Just in case."

"Shit," Chee said.

"These white men got you screwed," Largo said. "Face it. You file a complaint. What happens? Two *belacani* cops. One Navajo. The judge is *belacani*, too. And the Navajo cop is already under suspicion of getting off with the dope. What good does it do you? Go back in the Chuskas. Visit your folks. Get away from here."

"Yeah," Chee said. He was remembering Johnson's hand stinging across his face. He would take time off, but he wouldn't go to the Chuskas. Not yet.

"These drug police, they're hard people," Largo said. "Don't work by the rules. Do what they want to do. I don't know what they're going to do next. Neither do you. Take your time off. This isn't our business. Get out of the way. Don't tell anybody where you're going. Good idea not to."

"Okay," Chee said. "I won't." He walked to the door. "One other thing, Captain. Joseph Musket didn't show up for work at Burnt Water the day John Doe was killed and dumped up on the mesa. Not that day or the day before. I want to go to Santa Fe—to the state pen—and see what I can find out about Musket. Will you set it up?"

"I read your report this morning," Largo said. "You didn't mention that."

"I called Jake West later. After it was written."

"You think Musket is a witch?"

Largo might have smiled very faintly when he asked it. Chee wasn't sure.

"I just don't understand Musket," Chee said. He shrugged.

"I'll get a letter off today," Largo said. "Meanwhile you're on vacation. Get away from here. And remember this drug case is none of our business. It's a federal felony. Where it happened, it's Hopi reservation now, not joint jurisdiction. It doesn't concern Navajo Tribal Police. It doesn't concern Jim Chee." Largo paused and looked directly at Chee. "You hear me?"

"I hear you," Chee said.

13

$\blacklozenge$

It seemed to Chee, under the circumstances, that the wise and courteous thing to do was to make the telephone call from somewhere where there was no risk of Captain Largo's learning of it. He stopped at the Chevron station on the corner where the Tuba City road intersects with Arizona 160. He called the Hopi Cultural Center on Second Mesa.

Yes, Ben Gaines was registered at the motel. Chee let the telephone ring eight or nine times. Then placed the call again. Did they have a woman named Pauling registered? They did. She answered on the second ring.

"This is Officer Chee," Chee said. "You remember. The Navajo Tribal . . ."

"I remember you," Miss Pauling said.

"I'm trying to get hold of Ben Gaines," Chee said.

"I don't think he's in his room. The car he rented has been gone all day and I haven't seen him."

"When I talked to you, he wanted me to find a vehicle for him," Chee said. "Do you know if that's turned up yet?"

"Not that I've heard about. I don't think so."

"Would you tell Gaines I'm looking into it?"

"Okay," the woman said. "Sure."

Chee hesitated. "Miss Pauling?"

"Yes."

"Have you known Gaines a long time?"

There was a pause. "Three days," Miss Pauling said.

"Did your brother ever mention him?"

Another long pause.

"Look," Miss Pauling said. "I don't know what you're getting at. But no. That wasn't the sort of thing we talked about. I didn't know he had a lawyer."

"You think you should trust Gaines?"

In Chee's ear the telephone made a sound which might have passed for laughter. "You really are a policeman, aren't you," Miss Pauling said. "How do they teach you not to trust anybody?"

"Well," Chee said, "I was . . ."

"I know he knew my brother," Miss Pauling said. "And he called me and offered to help with everything. And then he came, and arranged to get the body brought back for the funeral, and told me what to do about getting a grave site in a national cemetery, and everything like that. Why shouldn't I trust him?"

"Maybe you should," Chee said.

Chee went home then. He put on his walking boots, got a fresh plastic gallon jug of ice out of the freezer and put it in his old canvas pack with a can of corned beef and a box of crackers. He stowed the bag and his bedroll behind the seat in his pickup and drove back down to the Chevron station. But instead of turning east toward New Mexico, the Chuska Mountains, and his family, he turned west and then southward on Navajo Route 3. Route 3 led past the cluster of Hopi stone huts which are Moenkopi village, into the Hopi Reservation, to Burnt Water Trading Post, and Wepo Wash, and that immensity of empty canyon country where a plane had crashed and a car might, or might not, have been hidden by a thin-faced man named Richard Palanzer.

14

◆

The first thing Chee learned about the missing vehicle was that someone—and Chee guessed it was the Drug Enforcement Agency—had already searched for it. Chee had worked his way methodically down from the crash site, checking every point where a wheeled vehicle could have left the wash bottom. Since the walls of the wash were virtually vertical and rarely rose less than eighteen to twenty feet, these possible exit points were limited to arroyos which fed the wash. Chee had checked each of them carefully for tire tracks. He found none, but at every arroyo there were signs that he wasn't the first to have looked. Two men had done it, two or three days earlier. They had worked together, not separately—a fact taught by noticing that sometimes the man wearing the almost new boots stepped on the other's tracks, and sometimes it worked the other way. From the nature of this hunt, Chee surmised that if the truck, or car, or whatever it was, was hidden out here anywhere, it had to be someplace where it couldn't be found from the air. Whoever was looking this hard would certainly have used an airplane. That narrowed things down.

When it became too dark to work, Chee rolled out his bedroll, dined on canned meat, crackers, and cold water. He got his book of U.S. Geological Survey Quadrangle Maps of Arizona out of his truck and turned to page 34, the Burnt Water Quadrangle. The thirty-two-mile-square section was reduced to a twenty-four-inch square, but provided a map scale at least twenty times larger than a road map, and the federal surveyors had marked in every detail of terrain, elevation, and drainage.

Chee sat on the sand with his back against the bumper, using the truck headlights for illumination. He checked each arroyo carefully, coordinating what the map showed him with his memory of the landscape. Behind him, there was a sudden pinging sound—the sound of the pickup engine cooling. From beyond the splash of yellow light formed by the truck lights, an owl screeched out its hunting call, again, and again, and then lapsed into silence. All quiet. And now, faint and far away, somewhere south toward the Hopi Mesas, the purr of an aircraft engine. From Chee's own knowledge, only three of the arroyos that fed Wepo Wash drained areas where a car might easily be hidden. He had already checked the mouth of one and found no tracks. The other two were downstream, both draining into the wash from the northwest, off the slopes of the great eroded hump with the misleading name Big Mountain. Both would lead high enough to get into the big brush and timber country and into the steeper slopes where you could expect to find undercuts and overhangs. In other words, where something as large as a car might be hidden. Tomorrow he would skip down the wash and check them both.

And, he thought, find absolutely nothing. He would find that whoever the DEA was using as a tracker had been there first and had also found nothing. There would be nothing to find. A plane had flown in with a load of dope and a car had come to meet it. The dope had been taken out of the plane and the car had driven away with it. Why keep it out here in the Painted Desert? The only answer Chee could think of to that question led him to Joseph Musket. If Musket was making the decisions, keeping it here would make sense. But Musket was a third-level, minor-league police character involved in a very big piece of business. Richard Palanzer would be the man making the decisions—or at least giving the orders. Why wouldn't Palanzer simply haul the load away to some familiar urban setting?

Or was he underestimating Joseph Musket? Was the young man they called Ironfingers more than he seemed to be? Was there a dimension in this which Chee hadn't guessed at? Chee considered the shooting of John Doe. Was this dead Navajo a loose end to something that Musket had taken the day off to tie up with a bullet? And if so, why leave the body out to be found? And why remove the parts a witch would use to make his corpse powder?

From the darkness beyond the range of the headlights he heard the sound of a dislodged pebble rolling down the wall of the wash. Then the sound of something scurrying. The desert was a nocturnal place—dead in the blinding light of sun but swarming with life in the darkness. Rodents came out of their burrows to feed on seeds, and the reptiles and other predators came out to hunt the rodents and each other. Chee yawned. From somewhere far back on Black Mesa he heard a coyote barking and from the opposite direction the faint purr of an aircraft engine. Chee reexamined the map, looking for anything he might have missed. His vandalized windmill was too new to have been marked, but the arroyo of the shrine was there. As Chee had guessed, it drained the slope of Second Mesa.

The plane was nearer now, its engine much louder. Chee saw its navigation lights low and apparently coming directly toward him. Why? Perhaps simple curiosity about why a car's lights would be burning out here. Chee scrambled to his feet, reached through the driver-side window, and flicked off the lights. A moment later the plane roared over, not a hundred yards off the ground. Chee stood for a moment, looking after it. Then he rerolled his blanket, and picked up his water jug, and walked up the arroyo. He found a place perhaps two hundred yards from the truck, where a cul-de-sac of smooth sand was screened from sight by a heavy growth of chamiso. He scooped out a depression for his hips, built a little mound of sand for his head, and rolled his blanket around this bed. Then he lay looking up at the stars. His uncle would tell him that wherever the car was driven, it was driven there for a reason. If it had been hidden out here, the act was a product of motivation. Chee could not think of what that motivation might be, but it must be there. If Palanzer had done this deed, as it seemed, he surely wouldn't have done it casually, without forethought and planning. He would have run for the city, for familiar territory, for a place where he could become quickly invisible, for a hideaway which he surely would have prepared. He'd want a safe place where he could keep the cargo until he could dispose of it. Hiding the car and the cargo out here made sense only if Musket was heavily involved. Musket must be involved. He would be the logical link between this isolated desert place and the narcotics business. Musket had been in the New Mexico prison on a narcotics conviction. He was a friend of West's son, probably he had visited here, probably he had seen Wepo Wash and remembered its possibilities as a very secret, utterly isolated landing strip. Musket had suggested it. Musket had used his old friendship to get a parolee job at Burnt Water so he could be on the site and complete the arrangements. That's where he had been when he was missing work at the trading post—up the wash, doing whatever had to be done to pave the way. But what in the world would there have been to do? Setting out the lanterns would have taken only a few minutes. Chee was worrying about that question when he drifted off to sleep.

He wasn't sure what awakened him. He was still on his back. Sometime during the night, without being aware of doing it, he had pulled the blanket partly over him. The air was chilly now. The stars overhead had changed. Mars and Jupiter had moved far down toward the western horizon and a late-rising slice of moon hung in the east. The darkness just before the dawn. He lay still, not breathing, straining to hear. He heard nothing. But a sort of memory of sound—a residue of whatever had awakened him—hung in his mind. Whatever it had been, it provoked fear.

He heard the sound of insects somewhere up the arroyo and down in Wepo Wash. Nothing at all nearby. That told him something. Something had quieted the insects. He could see nothing but the gray-green foliage of the chamiso bush, made almost black by the darkness. Then he heard the sighing sound of a breath exhaled. Someone was standing just beyond the bush, not eight feet away from him. Someone? Or something? A horse, perhaps? He'd noticed hoof marks in the wash bottom. And earlier he'd seen horses near the windmill. Horses tend to be noisy breathers. He strained to hear, and heard nothing. A man, most likely, just standing there on the other side of the bush. Why? Someone in the plane obviously had seen his truck. Had they come, or sent someone, to check on him?

Click. From just beyond the bush. Click. Click. Click. Click. A small metallic sound. Chee couldn't identify it. Metal against metal? And then another exhalation of breath, and the sound of feet moving on the sand. Footsteps moving down the arroyo toward its intersection with the wash. Toward Chee's truck.

Chee rolled off the bedroll, careful not to make a sound. His rifle was on the rack across the back window of the truck. His pistol was in its holster, locked in the glove box. He raised his head cautiously above the bush.

The man was walking slowly away from him. He could only presume it was a man. A large shape, a little darker than the darkness surrounding it, a sense of slow movement. Then the movement stopped. A light flashed on—a yellow beam probing the boulders along the wall of the arroyo. The moving light silhouetted first the legs of whoever held the flashlight, then the right arm and shoulder and the shape of a pistol held, muzzle down, in the right hand. Then the light flicked off again. In the renewed darkness Chee could see only the shape of the yellow light imprinted on his iris. The shape of the man was lost to him. He ducked behind the chamiso again, waiting for vision to return.

When it did, the arroyo was empty.

Chee waited for the first dim light before he made his move for his truck. His first impulse was to abandon it. To slip away in the darkness and make the long walk back to the Burnt Water Trading Post and thereby avoid the risk that the man who had hunted him in the darkness was waiting for him at the truck. But as time ticked away, the urgency and reality of the danger diminished with it. Within an hour, what his instincts had told him of danger had faded along with the adrenaline it had pumped into his blood. What had happened was easy enough to read. Someone interested in recovering the drugs had rented a plane to keep an eye on the area. Chee's lights had been seen. Someone had been sent to find him and learn what he was doing. The pistol in hand was easily explained. The hunter was seeking the unknown in a strange and lonely darkness. He was nervous. He would have seen Chee's rifle on its rear-window rack but he'd have had no way of knowing Chee's pistol was locked away.

Even so, Chee was cautious. He moved along the arroyo rim to a point where he could look down at the truck. He spent a quarter of an hour sitting in the shelter of the rocks there, watching for any sign of movement. All he saw was a burrowing owl returning from its nocturnal hunt to its hole in the bank across from him. The owl scouted the truck and the area around it. If it saw anything dangerous, it showed no sign of it until it saw Chee. Then it shied violently away. That was enough for Jim Chee. He got up and walked to the truck.

With his pistol back on his belt, Chee checked the area

85

around the arroyo mouth to confirm what the burrowing owl had told him. Nothing human was watching the area. Then he took a look at the tracks his hunter had left. The man wore boots with worn waffle soles, the same soles he'd noticed at the site of the crash. Someone in these same boots had placed the fatal lanterns. He'd approached the truck from downwash, left tracks all around it, and then walked almost a half mile up the arroyo and back again. Finally he'd left the way he had come.

Chee spent the rest of the morning examining the two downwash arroyos which the map suggested might have offered hiding places for a car. Nothing that left tire tracks had gone up either of them. He sat in the truck cab, finished the last of his crackers with the last of his water, and thought it all through again. Then he went back to both arroyos, walked a half mile up from their mouths, and made an intensive hands-and-knees spot check of likely places. Nothing. That eliminated the possibility that Palanzer, or Musket, or whoever was driving, had done a thorough and meticulous job of wiping out tracks at the turn-in point. With that out of the way, he drove back up to the arroyo where he'd spent the night.

Once it had been his favorite prospect. But he'd written it off, just as he had first written off the downstream arroyos when he'd found no trace of tracks at the mouth. Now he intended to be absolutely sure, and when he was finished, he would be equally sure that no car was hidden up Wepo Wash. Chee skipped the first hundred yards, which he'd already studied fruitlessly. Upstream the arroyo had cut through an extensive bed of hard-packed caliche. Here there were only occasional pockets of sand and Chee inspected those which couldn't have been avoided by a wheeled vehicle. He took his time. He found lizard tracks, and the trail left by a rattlesnake, the tiny paw marks of kangaroo rats, the marks left by birds and a variety of rodents. No tire marks. At a broad expanse of packed sand another hundred yards upstream, he made the same sort of check. Here he found a scratch curving across the sandy surface. Parallel with it were other lines, almost invisible. Chee squatted on his heels, looking. What had caused this? A porcupine might have dragged his tail across here. But this wasn't porcupine country. It would starve a porcupine.

Chee reached behind him, broke a limb off a growth of rabbit bush. He swept it across the sand. It produced a half-dozen scratches and a pattern of tiny parallel furrows. Chee examined them. Given a week for wind and gravity to soften their edges, these furrows would look much like what he had found. The sand had been swept.

Chee walked rapidly up-arroyo with hardly a glance at its bed. Sooner or later whoever had done the sweeping would have run out of time, or of patience, and decided enough had been done. About a thousand yards later, he found where that had happened.

He noticed the broom first. It was dried now, its color changed from its normal gray-green to gray-white, which made it instantly visible in the growth of healthy brush where it had been thrown. Chee salvaged it, inspected it, and confirmed that it had been used as a broom, then he tossed it away.

He found tire tracks at the next stretch of sand. They were faint, but they were unmistakable. Chee dropped to his hands and knees and studied the pattern of marks. He matched them in his memory with the tracks he had seen at the site of the wreckage. They were the same tread pattern.

Chee rocked back on his heels, pushed his hat off his forehead, and wiped away the sweat. He had found the invisible car. Unless it could fly, it was somewhere up this arroyo.

15

◆

After that there was no need for tracking. Chee paused only to check the few places where small gullies drained into the arroyo, places which might conceivably provide an exit route. He walked steadily up-arroyo toward the Black Mesa. The arroyo wound through increasingly rough country, its bed narrowing, becoming increasingly rocky and brush-choked. At places now the vehicle had left a trail of broken branches. Late in the afternoon, Chee heard the airplane again, droning miles away over the place where he had left his truck parked. When it approached up the arroyo he stood out of sight under an overhang of brush until it disappeared.

It was just sundown when he found the vehicle, and then he almost walked past it. He was tired. He was thirsty. He was thinking that within another hour it would be too dark to see. He saw not the vehicle itself but the broken brush it had left in its wake. Its driver had turned it up a narrow gully that fed the arroyo, forced it into a tangle of mountain mahogany and salt brush, and closed the growth as well as possible behind it.

It was a dark-green GMC carryall, apparently new. In a little while Chee would find out if it was loaded with cocaine, or perhaps with bales of currency intended to pay for cocaine. But there was no hurry. He took a moment to think. Then he scouted the area carefully, looking for tracks. If he could find the tracks of waffle soles and of cowboy boots, it would confirm what he already knew—that those men had driven away in the car he'd heard leaving. The area around the carryall was a mat of leaves and twigs, and the gully bottom was granular decomposed granite where it wasn't solid rock. Impossible for tracking. Chee found scuff marks but nothing he could identify.

The carryall was locked, its windows rolled all the way up, and totally fogged with interior moisture. With a sealed vehicle, some such fogging was usual, even in this arid climate, but these windows were opaque. There must be some source of moisture locked inside. Chee sat on a boulder and considered what to do.

Not only wasn't this his case; he'd been specifically warned away from it by the people whose case it was. Not only had he been warned off by the feds; Captain Largo had personally and specifically ordered him to keep clear of it. If he broke into the carryall, he'd be tampering with evidence.

Chee took out a cigaret, lit it, and exhaled a plume of smoke. The sun was down now, reflecting from a cloud formation over the desert to the south. It added a reddish tint to the light. To the northwest, a thundercloud that had been building over the Coconino Rim had reached the extreme altitude where its boiling upcurrents could no longer overcome the bitter cold and the thinness of the air. Its top had flattened and been spread by stratospheric winds into a vast fan of ice crystals. The sunset striped the cloud in three color zones. The top several thousand feet were dazzling white—still reflecting the direct sunlight and forming a blinding contrast against the dark-blue sky. Lower, the cloud mass was illuminated by reflected light. It was a thousand shades of pink, rose, even salmon. And below that, where not even reflected light could reach, the color ranged from dirty gray to blue-black. There, lightning flickered. In the Hopi villages the people were calling the clouds. It was already raining on the Coconino Rim. And the storm was moving eastward, as summer storms always did. With any luck, rain would be falling here within two hours. Just a little rain—just a shower—would wipe out tracks in this sandy country. But Chee was desert-bred. He never really believed rain would fall.

He took a long drag off the cigaret, savored the taste of the smoke, exhaled it slowly through his nostrils, watched the blue haze dissipate. He was thinking of Chee in the grand jury room, under oath, the assistant U.S. District Attorney staring at him. "Officer Chee, I want to remind you of the penalty for perjury; for lying under oath. Now I want to ask you directly: Did you, or did you not, locate the GMC carryall in which . . ." Chee switched from that thought to another. The memory of Johnson smiling at him, Johnson's hand stinging across his face, Johnson's voice, threatening. Anger returned, and shame. He inhaled another lungful of smoke, putting anger aside. Anger was beside the point. The point was the puzzle. Here before his eyes was another piece of it. Chee stubbed out the cigaret. He puts the remains carefully in his pocket.

Jimmying the wing window would have been easy with a screwdriver. With Chee's knife it took longer. Even shaded as the vehicle was, the day's heat had built up inside, and when the leverage of the steel blade broke the seal, pressurized air escaped with a sighing sound. The odor surprised him. It was a strong chemical smell. The heavy, sickish smell of disinfectant. Chee slid his hand through the wing, flicked up the lock, and opened the door.

Richard Palanzer was sitting on the back seat. Chee recognized him instantly from the photograph Cowboy had shown him. He was a smallish white man, with rumpled iron-gray hair, close-set eyes, and a narrow bony face over which death and desiccation had drawn the skin tight. He was wearing a gray nylon jacket, a white shirt, and cowboy boots. He leaned stiffly against the corner of the back seat, staring blindly at the side window.

Chee looked at him through the open door, engulfed by the escaping stench of disinfectant. The smell was Lysol, Chee guessed. Lysol fog and death. Chee's stomach felt queasy. He controlled it. There was something funny about the man's left eye, an odd sort of distortion. Chee eased himself into the front seat, careful of what he touched. At close range he could see the man's left contact lens had slipped down below the pupil. Apparently he had been shot where he sat. On the left side, from just above the waist, both jacket and trousers were black with dried blood, and the same blackness caked the seat and the floor mat.

Chee searched the carryall, careful not to smudge old fingerprints or to leave new ones. The glove box was unlocked. It contained an operating manual and the rental papers from the Hertz office at Phoenix International Airport. The vehicle had been rented to Jansen. Cigaret butts in the ashtray. Nothing else. No bundles of hundred-dollar bills. No great canvas sacks filled with dope. Nothing except the corpse of Richard Palanzer.

Chee rolled the side vent shut as tightly as he could, reset the door lock and slammed it shut. The vehicle was left exactly as he had found it. A careful cop would notice the vent had been forced, but maybe there wouldn't be a careful cop on the job. Maybe there wouldn't be any reason for suspicion. Or maybe there would be. Either way, there was nothing he could do about it. And if the pattern continued, he could count on the feds screwing things up.

He walked back down the arroyo in the thickening darkness. He was tired. He was nauseated. He was sick of death. He wished he knew a lot more than he did about Joseph Musket. Now he was all there was left. Ironfingers alive, and four men dead, and a fortune in narcotics missing.

"Ironfingers, where are you?" Chee said.

16

◆

The man who answered the telephone at the Coconino County Sheriff's Office in Flagstaff said wait a minute and he'd check. The minute stretched into three or four. And then the man reported that Deputy Sheriff Albert Dashee was supposed to be en route to Moenkopi—which was good news for Jim Chee since Moenkopi was only a couple of miles from the telephone booth he was calling from, at the Tuba City Chevron station. He climbed into his pickup truck, and rolled down U.S. 160 to the intersection of Navajo 3. He pulled off at a place from which he could look down into the patchy Hopi cornfields along the bottom of Moenkopi Wash and onto the little red stone villages, and at every possible route Cowboy Dashee could take if he was going anywhere near Moenkopi. Chee turned off the ignition, and waited. While he waited he rehearsed what he would say to Cowboy, and how he would say it.

Cowboy's white patrol car drove by, stopped, backed up, stopped again beside Chee's truck.

"Hey, man," Cowboy said. "I thought you were on vacation."

"That was yesterday," Chee said. "Today I'm wondering if you've caught your windmill vandal yet."

"One of the Gishis," Cowboy said. "I know it. You know it. Everybody knows it. Trouble is, all Navajos look alike, so we don't know who to arrest."

"In other words, no luck. No progress," Chee said.

Cowboy turned off his ignition, lit a cigaret, relaxed. "Tell you the truth," he said, "I been sort of laying back on that one. Wanted to see how you could do with not much help."

"Or maybe not any help?"

Cowboy laughed. He shook his head. "Nobody's ever going to catch that son of a bitch," he said. "How you going to catch him? No way."

"How about your big drug business?" Chee said. "Doing any good?"

"Nothing," Cowboy said. "Not that I know of, anyway. But that's a biggy. The sheriff and the undersheriff, they're handling that one themselves. Too big a deal for just a deputy."

"They take you off of it?"

"Oh, no," Cowboy said. "Sheriff had me in yesterday, wanting me to tell him where they had the stuff hid. He figured I'm Hopi, and it happened on the Hopi Reservation, so I gotta know."

"If it happened in Alaska, he'd ask an Eskimo," Chee said.

"Yeah," Cowboy said. "I just told him you probably got off with it. Reminded him you were out there when it happened, had your truck and all. They ought to look in the back of your truck."

The conversation was going approximately in the direction Chee wanted to take it. He adjusted it slightly.

"I think they already have," he said. "I didn't tell you about the DEA people talking to me. They had about the same idea."

Cowboy looked startled. "Hell they did," he said. "Seriously?"

"Sounded serious," Chee said. "Serious enough so Largo reminded me about Navajo Police not having jurisdiction. Warned me to stay completely away from it."

"He don't want you distracted from our windmill,"

Cowboy said. "The crime of the century."

"Trouble is, I think I can guess where they put that car the feds are looking for."

Cowboy looked at him. "Oh, yeah?"

"It's up one of those arroyos. If it's out there at all, that's where it is."

"No it ain't," Cowboy said. "The sheriff was talking about that. The DEA and the FBI had that idea, too. They checked them all."

Chee laughed.

"I know what you mean," Cowboy said. "But I think they did a pretty good job this time. Looked on the ground, and flew up and down 'em in an airplane."

"If you were hiding a car, you'd hide it where an airplane couldn't see it. Under an overhang. Under a tree. Cover it up with brush."

"Sure," Cowboy said. He was looking at Chee thoughtfully, his elbow propped on the sill of the car window, chin resting on the heel of his hand. "What makes you think you could find it?"

"Look here," he said, motioning to Cowboy. He dug his Geological Survey map book out from beneath the seat.

Cowboy climbed out of his patrol car and climbed into Chee's truck. "I need me a book of those," he said. "But the sheriff would be too tight to pay for 'em."

"You're hiding a car," Chee said. "Okay. God knows why, but you're hiding it. And you know the law's going to be looking for it. The law has airplanes, helicopters, all that. So you've got to get it someplace where it can't be seen from the air."

Cowboy nodded.

"So what do you have?" Chee ran his finger down the crooked blue line which marked Wepo Wash on the map. "He drove down the wash. No tracks going up. Personally,

94

I'd bet he drove right down here to where it goes under the highway bridge, and then drove off to Los Angeles. But the feds don't think so, and the feds have got some way of knowing things they aren't telling us Indians about. So maybe he did hide his car. So where did he hide it? It's not in the wash. I'd have seen it. Maybe you'd have seen it." Chee made a doubtful face. "Maybe even the feds would have seen it. So it's not in the wash. And it's somewhere between where the plane crashed and the highway. Gives you twenty-five miles or so. And it gives you three arroyos which are cut back into country where you've got enough brush and trees and overhang so you could hide a car." He pointed out the three, and glanced at Cowboy.

Cowboy was interested. He leaned over the map, studying it.

"You agree?"

"Yeah," Cowboy said slowly. "Those other ones don't go anywhere."

"These two lead back into the Big Mountain Mesa," Chee said. "This one leads into Black Mesa. In fact, it leads back up toward Kisigi Spring. Back up toward where we found John Doe's body dumped."

Cowboy was studying the map. "Yeah," he said.

"So if Largo hadn't promised to break my arm and fire me if I didn't stay away from this, that's where I'd be looking."

"Trouble is, they already looked," Cowboy said. But he didn't sound convinced.

"I can see it. They drive along the wash and when they get to an arroyo, somebody gets out and looks around for tire tracks. They don't find any, so he climbs back in and drives along to the next one. Right?"

"Yeah," Cowboy said.

"So if you're going to hide the car, what do you do? You

think that if you leave tracks they're going to just follow them and find you. So you turn up the arroyo, and you get out, and you take your shirttail or something, and you brush out your tracks for a little ways."

Cowboy was looking at Chee.

"I don't know how hard the feds looked," Cowboy said. "Sometimes they're not the smartest bastards in the world."

"Look," Chee said. "If by chance that car does happen to be hidden out in one of those arroyos, you damn sure better keep quiet about this. Largo'd fire my ass. He was sore. He said I wasn't going to get a second warning."

"Hell," Cowboy said. "He wouldn't fire you."

"I mean it," Chee said. "Leave me out of it."

"Hell," Cowboy said. "I'm like you. That car's long gone by now."

It was time to change the subject. "You got any windmill ideas for me?" Chee asked.

"Nothing new," Cowboy said. "What you've got to do is convince Largo that there's no way to protect that windmill short of putting three shifts of guards on it." He laughed. "That, or getting a transfer back to Crownpoint."

Chee turned on the ignition. "Well, I better get moving."

Cowboy opened the door, started to get out, stopped. "Jim," he said. "You already found that car?"

Chee produced a chuckle. "You heard what I said. Largo said keep away from that case."

Cowboy climbed out and closed the door behind him. He leaned on the sill, looking in at Chee. "And you wouldn't do nothing that the captain told you not to?"

"I'm serious, Cowboy. The DEA climbed all over Largo. They think I was out there that night to meet the plane. They think I know where that dope shipment is. I'm not kidding you. It's absolutely goddamn none of my business. I'm staying away from it."

Cowboy climbed into his patrol car, started the engine.

96

He looked back at Chee. "What size boots you wear?"

Chee frowned. "Tens."

"Tell you what I'll do," Cowboy said. "If I see any size ten footprints up that arroyo, I'll just brush 'em out!"

17

◆

Black Mesa is neither black nor a mesa. It is far too large for that definition—a vast, broken plateau about the size and shape of Connecticut. It is virtually roadless, almost waterless, and uninhabited except for an isolated scattering of summer herding camps. It rises out of the Painted Desert more than seven thousand feet. A dozen major dry washes and a thousand nameless arroyos drain away runoff from its bitter winters and the brief but torrential "male rains" of the summer thunderstorm season. It takes its name from the seams of coal exposed in its towering cliffs, but its colors are the grays and greens of sage, rabbit brush, juniper, cactus, grama and bunch grass, and the dark green of creosote brush, mesquite, piñon, and (in the few places where springs flow) pine and spruce. It is a lonely place even in grazing season and has always been territory favored by the Holy People of the Navajo and the kachinas and guarding spirits of the Hopis. Masaw, the bloody-faced custodian of the Fourth World of the Hopis, specifically instructed various clans of the Peaceful People to return there when they completed their epic migrations and to live on the three mesas which extend like great gnarled fingers from Black Mesa's southern ramparts. Its craggy cliffs are the eagle-collection grounds of the Hopi Flute, Side Corn, Drift Sand, Snake, and Water clans. It is dotted with shrines and holy places. For Chee's people it was an integral part of Dinetah, where

Changing Woman taught the Dinee they must live in the beauty of the Way she and the Holy People taught them.

Chee was familiar with only a little of the eastern rim of this sprawling highland. As a boy, he had been taken westward by Hosteen Nakai from Many Farms into the Blue Gap country to collect herbs and minerals at the sacred places for the Mountain Way ceremony. Once they had gone all the way into Dzilidushzhinih Peaks, the home of Talking God himself, to collect materials for Hosteen Nakai's *jish*, the bundle of holy things a shaman must have to perfect his curing rituals. But Dzilidushzhinih was far to the east. The camp of Fannie Musket, the mother of Joseph Musket, was near the southern edge of the plateau, somewhere beyond the end of the trail that wandered southward from the Cottonwood day school toward Balakai Point. It was new country to Chee, without landmarks that meant anything to him, and he'd stopped at the trading post at Cottonwood to make sure the directions he'd gotten earlier made sense. The skinny white woman running the place had penciled him a map on the page of a Big Chief writing tablet. "If you stay on that track that leads past Balakai arroyo you can't miss it," the woman said. "And you can't get off the track or you'll tear the bottom outa your truck." She laughed. "Matter of fact, if you're not careful you tear it out even if you stay on the track." On his way out Chee noticed "Fannie Musket" scrawled in chalk on the red paint of a new fifty-gallon oil drum which sat on the porch beside the front door. He went back in.

"This barrel belong to the Muskets?"

"Hey," the woman said. "That's a good idea. You want to haul that out for them? They're dried up out there and they're hauling water and they had me get 'em another drum."

"Sure," Chee said. He loaded it into the back of his pickup, rolled the truck to the overhead tank that held the post's water supply, rinsed out the drum, and filled it.

"Tell Fannie I put the barrel on her pawn ticket," the woman said. "I'll put the water on there, too."

"I'll get the water," Chee said.

"Two dollars," the woman said. She shook her head. "If it don't rain we ain't going to have any to sell."

Fannie Musket was glad to get the water. She helped Chee rig the block and tackle to lift the barrel onto a plank platform where two other such barrels sat. One was empty and when Chee tapped his knuckles against the other, the sound suggested no more than ten gallons left.

"Getting hard to live out here," Mrs. Musket said. "Seems like it don't rain anymore." She glanced up at the sky, which was a dark, clear blue with late summer's usual scattering of puffy clouds building up here and there. By midafternoon they would have built up to a vain hope of a thundershower. By dark, both clouds and hope would have dissipated.

Chee and Mrs. Musket had introduced themselves, by family, by kinship, and by clan. (She was Standing Rock, born for the Mud Clan.) He had told Mrs. Musket that he hoped she would talk to him about her son.

"You are hunting for him," she said. Navajo is a language which loads its meanings into its verbs. She used the word which means "to stalk," as a hunted animal, and not the form which means "to search for," as for someone lost. The tone was as accusing as the word.

Chee changed the verb. "I search for him," Chee said. "But I know I will not find him here. I am told he is a smart man. He would not come here while we search for him, and even if he had, I would not ask his mother to tell me where to find him. I just want to learn what kind of a man he is."

"He is my son," Mrs. Musket said.

"Did he come home after they let him out of the prison? Before he went to work at Burnt Water?"

"He came home. He wanted to have an Enemy Way done

100

for him. He went to see Tallman Begay and hired Hosteen Begay to be the singer for it. And then after the sing, he went to Burnt Water."

"It was the right thing to do," Chee said. It was exactly what he would have done himself. Purified himself from prison, and all the hostile, alien ways the prison represented. The character of Joseph Musket took on a new dimension.

"Why do you come to ask me questions this time? Before, another policeman came."

"That's because the police station at Chinle is closer," Chee explained. "A policeman came from there to save money and time."

"Then why do you come now?"

"Because there are many odd things about that burglary," Chee said. "Many questions I can't answer. I am curious."

"Do you know my son did not steal that pawn?"

"I don't know who stole it," Chee said.

"I know he didn't. Do you know why? Because he had money!" Mrs. Musket said it triumphantly. The ultimate proof.

"There are people among the *belacani* who steal even when they don't need to steal," Chee said.

Mrs. Musket's expression was skeptical. The concept was totally foreign to her.

"He had hundred-dollar bills," she said. "Many of them." She held up six fingers. "And other money in his purse. Twenty-dollar bills." She looked at Chee quizzically, waiting for him to concede that no one with hundred-dollar bills could be suspected of stealing. Certainly no Navajo would be likely to.

"He had this money when he first got here?"

Mrs. Musket nodded. "He wrote us that he was coming and my husband took the pickup truck on the day and drove out to Window Rock to meet the bus. He had all that money then."

Chee was trying to remember what prisoners were given

when they left the penitentiary. Twenty dollars, he thought. That and whatever they might have in the canteen fund. A maximum of another fifty dollars, he suspected.

"It doesn't sound like he would steal the jewelry if he had all that money," Chee said. "But where did he go? Why doesn't he talk to us and tell us he didn't steal it?"

Mrs. Musket wasn't going to answer that question. Not directly at least. Finally she said, "They put him in prison once."

"Why was that?"

"He made bad friends," Mrs. Musket said.

Chee asked for a drink of water, got it, drank it, changed the subject. They talked of desperate difficulties of sheep-herding in a drought. All her sons-in-law were out with their herds, as was her husband, and now they had to drive them so far for grass and water that they could not return to their hogans at night. The women took them food. And already they had lost eleven lambs and even some of the ewes were dying. With Chee guiding it, the conversation gradually edged back to Joseph Musket. He had always been good with sheep. A careful hand with the shears, adept at castration. Reliable. A good boy. Even when he had been thrown from his horse and smashed his fingers and had to wear metal splints for so long, he could still shear faster than most young men. And he had told her that when he finished working at Burnt Water—by the end of summer—he would have plenty of money to buy his own herd. A big herd. He planned to buy two hundred ewes. But first he would go to all the squaw dances, find himself a young woman to marry. Someone whose family had plenty of grazing rights.

"He said that after he worked for the trading post a little while he didn't want to have anything else to do with the white men after that," Mrs. Musket said. "He said he only had one white man who had ever been a friend, and that all the others just got you in trouble."

"Did he say who the friend was?"

"It was a boy he knew when he went to the Cottonwood school," Mrs. Musket said. "I can't remember what he called him."

"Was it West?" Chee asked.

"West," Mrs. Musket said. "I think so."

"Does he have any other friends? Navajo friends?"

Mrs. Musket examined Chee thoughtfully. "Just some young men around here," she said vaguely. "Maybe some friends he made when he was away with the white people. I don't think so."

Chee could think of nothing more to ask. Not with any hope of getting an answer. He gave Mrs. Musket the message about the cost of the water barrel being added to her pawn ticket and climbed back in the truck.

Mrs. Musket stood in the yard of the hogan, watching him. Her hands clasped together at her waist, twisting nervously.

"If you find him," she said, "tell him to come home."

18

Chee spent the next day as Largo had arranged, a long way from Tuba City and Wepo Wash. He drove fifty miles north toward the Utah border to see a woman named Mary Joe Natonabah about her complaint that her grazing on Twenty-nine Mile Wash was being trespassed by somebody else's sheep. She identified the trespasser as an old man called Largewhiskers Begay, who had his camp in the Yondots Mountains. That took Chee to Cedar Ridge Trading Post and down the horrible dirt road which leads westward toward the Colorado River gorge. He found the Begay camp, but not Largewhiskers, who had gone to Cameron to see about something or other. The only person at the camp was a surly young man with his arm in a cast, who identified himself as the son-in-law of Largewhiskers Begay. Chee told this young man of the Natonabah complaint, warned him of the consequences of violating another person's grazing right, and told him to tell Largewhiskers he'd be back one day to check it all out. By then it was noon. Chee's next job took him to Nipple Butte, where a man named Ashie McDonald had reportedly beaten up his cousin. Chee found the camp but not Ashie McDonald. McDonald's mother-in-law reported that he'd got a ride down to Interstate 40 and was hitchhiking into Gallup to visit some relatives. The mother-in-law claimed to know nothing of any beating, any fight, any cousin. By then it was a little after 4:40 P.M. Chee

was now sixty miles as the raven flew, ninety miles by un-
paved back roads, or 130 miles via the paved highway from
his trailer at Tuba City. He took the more direct dirt route.
It wandered northeast across the Painted Desert, past New-
berry Mesa, and Garces Mesa, and Blue Point, and Padilla
Mesa. The country was dead with drought, no sign of sheep,
no trace of green. He was off duty now, and he drove slowly,
thinking what he would do. This route would take him
through the Hopi villages of Oraibi, Hotevilla, and Bacobi,
and near the Hopi Cultural Center. He would stop at the
café there for his supper. He would learn if Ben Gaines
was still in the motel, or the Pauling woman. If Gaines was
there, Chee would see what he could learn from him. Maybe
he would tell Gaines where to find the car. Most likely he
wouldn't. Cowboy had two days to get there and find it,
but maybe something had interfered. Most likely he
wouldn't risk telling Gaines yet. He'd tell him only enough
to determine if he could learn anything from the lawyer.

The parking area at the Hopi Cultural Center held about
a dozen vehicles—more than usual, Chee guessed, because
the upcoming ceremonials were beginning to draw tourists.
Or was it that a missing cocaine shipment was beginning
to draw in the hunters? Before he parked, Chee circled the
motel, looking for the car Gaines had been driving. He didn't
find it.

In the restaurant he took a table beside one of the west
windows, ordered a bowl of what the menu called Hopi
Stew, and coffee. The Hopi girl who served it was maybe
twenty, and pretty, with her hair cut in the short bangs
that old-fashioned Hopis wore. She had dazzled the group
of tourists at the next table with her smile. With Chee, she
was strictly business. The Hopi dealing with the Navajo.
Chee sipped his coffee, and studied the other dining room
patrons, and thought of the nature of the drought, and where
Ironfingers Musket might be, and of ethnic antagonisms.

This one was part abstraction, built into the Hopi legends of warfare: The enemy killed by the Hopi Twin War Gods were Navajo, as the enemy killed by the Navajo Holy People were Utes, or Kiowas, or Taos Indians. But the long struggle over the Joint Use Reservation lands lent a sort of reality to the abstraction in the minds of some. Now, at last, the U.S. Supreme Court had ruled, and the Hopis had won, and 9,000 Navajos were losing the only homes their families could remember. And the anger lingered, even among the winners. The windowpane beside him reflected red. The sun had gone down behind the San Francisco Peaks and turned the bottom of the clouds that hung over it a luminous salmon-pink. The mountain, too, was contested territory. For the Hopis, it was Mount Sinai itself—the home of the kachina spirits from August until February, when they left this world and returned underground where the spirits live. For Chee's people it was also sacred. It was Evening Twilight Mountain, one of the four mountains First Man had built to mark the corners of Dinetah. It was the Mountain of the West, the home of the great *yei* spirit, Abalone Girl, and the place where the Sacred Bear of Navajo legend had been so critically wounded by the Bow People that the ritual songs described him as being "fuzzy with arrows"—verbal imagery which had caused Chee as a child to think of the spirit as looking like a gigantic porcupine. The mountain now was outlined blue-black against a gaudy red horizon and the beauty of it lifted Chee's mood.

"Mr. Chee."

Miss Pauling was standing beside his table.

Chee stood.

"No. Don't get up. I wanted to talk to you."

"Why don't you join me?" Chee said.

"Thank you," she said. She looked tired and worried. It would be better, Chee thought, if she looked frightened. She shouldn't be here. She should have gone home. He signaled for the waitress. "I can recommend the stew," he said.

"Have you seen Mr. Gaines?" she asked.

"No," Chee said. "I haven't tried his room, but I didn't see his car."

"He's not here," she said. "He's been gone since yesterday morning."

"Did he say where he was going?" Chee asked. "Or when he'd be back?"

"Nothing," Miss Pauling said.

The waitress came. Miss Pauling ordered stew. The reflection from the fiery sunset turned her face red, but it looked lined and old.

"You should go home," Chee said. "Nothing you can do here."

"I want to find out who killed him," she said.

"You'll find out. Sooner or later the DEA, or the FBI, they'll catch them."

"Do you think so?" Miss Pauling asked. The tone suggested she doubted it.

So did Chee. "Well, probably not," he said.

"I want you to help me find out," she said. "Just whatever you can tell me. Like things that the police know that don't get into the newspapers. Do they have any suspects? Surely they must. Who do they suspect?"

Chee shrugged. "At one time they suspected a man named Palanzer. Richard Palanzer. I think he was one of the people the dope was being delivered to."

"Richard Palanzer," Miss Pauling said, as if she was memorizing it.

"However," Chee said. He stopped. He'd been out of touch all day. Had Cowboy found the car? Was it known that Palanzer was no longer a suspect? Almost certainly.

"He was flying in narcotics, then," Miss Pauling said. "Is that what they think?"

"Seems to be," Chee said.

"And Palanzer was supposed to pay for it, and instead he killed him. Was that the way it went? Who is this Palanzer? Where does he live? I know there are times when the police know who did something but they can't find the evidence to prove it. I'd just like to know who did it."

"Why?" Chee asked. He wanted to know, too, because he was curious. But that wasn't her reason.

"Because I loved him," she said. "That's the trouble. I really loved him."

The stew arrived. Miss Pauling stirred it absently. "There was no reason for killing him," she said, watching the spoon. "They could have just pointed a gun at him and he would have given it to them with no trouble at all. He would have just thought it was funny."

"I guess they didn't know that," Chee said.

"He was always such a happy boy," she said. "Everything was fun for him. I'm five years older and when our mother left . . . You know how it is—I sort of took care of him until Dad remarried."

Chee said nothing. He was wondering why it was so important for her to know who was to blame. There was a puzzle here to be solved, but after that, what did it matter?

"There was no reason to kill him," she said. "And whoever did it is going to suffer for it." She said it with no particular emphasis, still moving the spoon mechanically through the well-stirred stew. "They're not going to kill him and just walk away from it."

"But sometimes they do," Chee said. "That's the way it is."

"No," she said. The tone was suddenly vehement. "They won't get away with it. You understand that?"

"Not exactly," Chee said.

"Do you understand 'An eye for an eye, a tooth for a tooth'?"

"I've heard it," Chee said.

"Don't you believe in justice? Don't you believe that things need to be evened up?"

Chee shrugged. "Why not?" he said. As a matter of fact, the concept seemed as strange to him as the idea that someone with money would steal had seemed to Mrs. Musket. Someone who violated basic rules of behavior and harmed you was, by Navajo definition, "out of control." The "dark wind" had entered him and destroyed his judgment. One avoided such persons, and worried about them, and was pleased if they were cured of this temporary insanity and returned again to *hozro*. But to Chee's Navajo mind, the idea of punishing them would be as insane as the original act. He understood it was a common attitude in the white culture, but he'd never before encountered it so directly.

"That's really what I want to talk to you about," Miss Pauling said. "If this Palanzer did it, I want to know it and I want to know where to find him. If somebody else was responsible, I want to know that." She paused. "I can pay you."

Chee looked doubtful.

"I know you say you're not working on this. But you're the one who found out how he was killed. And you're the only one I know."

"I tell you what I'll do," Chee said. "You go home. If I can find out whether Palanzer is the one, I'll call you and tell you. And then if I can find out where you could look for Palanzer, I'll let you know that, too."

"That's all I can ask," she said.

"Then you'll go home?"

"Gaines has the tickets," she said. "It was all so sudden. He called me at work, and told me about the crash and arranged to meet me. And he said he was Robert's lawyer and we should fly right out and see about it. So he took me home and I put some things in a bag and we went right out to the airport and all the money I have is just what was in my purse."

"You have a credit card?" Chee asked. She nodded. "Use that. I'll get you a ride to Flagstaff."

Two men at a table near the cash register had been watching them. One was about thirty—a big man with long blond hair and small eyes under bushy blond eyebrows. The other, much older, had thin white hair and a suntanned face. His pin-striped three-piece suit looked out of place on Second Mesa.

"Do you know who Gaines is?" Chee asked.

"You mean besides being my brother's attorney? Well, I guess from what I hear that he must be somebody involved in this drug business. I guess that's the real reason he wanted me along." She chuckled, without humor. "To make him legitimate in dealing with people. Is that right?"

"So it would seem," Chee said.

Cowboy Dashee came through the walkway, paused a moment by the cash register, spotted Chee, and came over.

"Saw you parked out there," he said.

"This is Deputy Sheriff Albert Dashee," Chee said. "Miss Pauling is the sister of the pilot of that plane."

Cowboy nodded. "Everybody calls me Cowboy," he said. He pulled a chair over from an adjoining table and sat down.

"Why don't you pull up a chair and join us?" Chee asked.

"You know this guy's a Navajo?" he asked Miss Pauling. "Sometimes he tries to pass himself off as one of us."

Miss Pauling managed a smile.

"What's new?" Chee asked.

"You talked to your office this afternoon?"

"No," Chee said.

"You haven't heard about finding the car, or turning up the necklace?"

"Necklace?"

"From the Burnt Water burglary. Big squash blossom job.

110

Girl over at Mexican Water pawned it."

"Where'd she get it?"

"Who else?" Cowboy said. "Joseph Musket. Old Ironfingers playing Romeo." Cowboy turned to Miss Pauling. "Shop talk," he said. "Mr. Chee and I have been worrying about this burglary and now a piece of the loot finally turned up."

"When?" Chee asked. "How'd it happen?"

"She just pawned it yesterday," Cowboy said. "Said she met this guy at a squaw dance over there somewhere, and he wanted to . . ." Cowboy flushed slightly, glanced at Miss Pauling. "Anyway, he got romantic and he gave her the necklace."

"And it was Ironfingers."

"That's what she said his name was." Cowboy grinned at Chee. "I notice with intense surprise that you're not interested in the car."

"You said you found it?"

"That's right," Cowboy said. "Just followed a sort of hunch I had. Followed up an arroyo out there and believe it or not, there it was—hidden up under some bushes."

"Good for you," Chee said.

"I'll tell you what's good for me," Cowboy said. "I jimmied my way into it through the vent on the right front window, pried it right open."

"That's the best way to get in," Chee said.

"I thought you'd say that," Cowboy said.

Miss Pauling was watching them curiously.

Chee turned to her.

"You remember me telling you that the plane crash and the narcotics case wasn't my business? Well, it's in the jurisdiction of Mr. Dashee's sheriff's department. Coconino County. And now Cowboy has found that car that everyone's been wondering about. The one that drove away from the plane crash."

"Oh," she said. "Can you tell us about it?"

Cowboy looked slightly doubtful. He glanced at Chee again. "Well," he said. "I guess so. Not much to tell, really. Green GMC carryall. Somebody drove it way up that arroyo and jammed it under the brush where it couldn't be seen. Been rented at Phoenix to that guy Jansen—the one that was found out there by the plane crash. Bloodstains on the back seat. Nothing in it. I think the FBI's out there now, checking it for fingerprints and so forth."

"Nothing in it?" Chee said. He hoped he'd kept the surprise out of his voice. Cowboy looked at him.

"Few butts in the ashtray. Rental papers in the glove box. Owner's manual. No big bundles labeled cocaine. Nothing like that. I guess we'll be hunting around there tomorrow."

Chee became aware that Miss Pauling was staring at him.

"You all right?" she asked.

"I'm fine," Chee said.

"Funny thing," Cowboy said. "The inside had a funny smell. Like disinfectant. I wonder why that would be."

"Beats me," Chee said.

Chee considered it as he drove back to Tuba City. Obviously the body had been gone when Cowboy found the vehicle. Obviously someone had come and taken it. Why? Perhaps because whoever had seen him parked at the arroyo mouth had become nervous and decided the body might be found. But why preserve it in the first place? And who had moved it? Joseph Musket, it would seem. But tonight he felt very disappointed in Ironfingers. Disillusioned. Musket should be smarter than the run-of-the-mill thief. In his mind Chee had built him up to be much too clever to do the same thing that always trips up small-time thieves. And the facts as Chee knew them seemed to make him too smart to give a girl that stolen necklace. Someone seemed to have thought so. Someone had given him something close to seven hundred dollars—probably, Chee guessed, an even thousand—to do something when he left the prison at Santa

112

Fe. And whatever it was, it involved working until the end of summer at Burnt Water. Doing what? Setting up and watching the landing strip for a multimillion-dollar narcotics delivery. That seemed to be the answer. But if he had seven hundred dollars in his pocket, if he had coming a payoff big enough to buy a wealth in sheep, why would he steal the pawn jewelry? Chee had been over all of that before, and the only motive he could think of was to provide what would seem to be a logical reason for disappearing from the trading post. Something which might put off the hunters if he intended to steal the shipment. And that meant he was too damn smart to give an instantly identifiable piece of squash blossom jewelry to some girl he'd picked up.

"Ironfingers, where are you?" Chee asked the night.

And oddly, just as he said it, aloud, to himself, another little mystery solved itself in his mind. He knew suddenly what had caused the clicking sound he'd heard in the darkness on the other side of the chamiso bushes. To make certain, he slid his .38 out of its holster. With his thumb he moved the hammer back and forth—off safety, to full cock, and back to safety. Click. Click. Click. He glanced at the pistol and back at the highway again. It was the kind of nervous thing a man might do if he was tensely ready to shoot something. Or someone.

The thought of Musket, pistol cocked, hunting him in the dark aroused a surprising anger in Chee. It made the abstraction intensely personal. Well, Largo wanted him away from Tuba City. He'd quit postponing that trip to the prison in New Mexico. He'd take another step down the trail of Ironfingers.

19

The drive from Tuba City to the New Mexico State Penitentiary on the Santa Fe plateau is about four hundred miles. Chee, who had risen even earlier than usual and cheated a little on the speed limit, got there in the early afternoon. He identified himself through the microphone at the entrance tower and waited while the tower checked with someone in the administration building. Then the exterior gate slid open. When it had closed behind him, and locked itself, another motor purred and the inside gate rolled down its track. Jim Chee was inside the fence, walking up the long, straight concrete walk through the great flat emptiness of the entrance yard. Nothing living was visible except for a flight of crows high to the north, between the prison and the mountains. But the long rows of cell block windows stared at him. Chee looked back, conscious of being watched. Above the second-floor windows of the second block to his right, the gray concrete was smudged with black. That would be cell block 3, Chee guessed, where more than thirty convicts were butchered and burned by their fellow prisoners in the ghastly riot of 1980. Had Joseph Musket been here then? If he'd been among the rioters, he'd concealed his role well enough to justify parole.

Another electronic lock let Chee through the door of the administration building, into the presence of a thin, middle-aged Chicano guard who manned the entrance desk. "Navajo Tribal Police," the guard said, eyeing Chee curiously. He glanced down at his clipboard. "Mr. Armijo will handle you." Another guard, also gray, also Chicano, led him wordlessly to Mr. Armijo's office.

Mr. Armijo was not wordless. He was plump, and perhaps forty, with coarse black hair razor-cut and blow-dried into this year's popular shape. His teeth were very, very white and he displayed them in a smile. "Mr. Chee. You're not going to believe this, but I know this Joseph Musket personally." Armijo's smile became a half inch broader. "He was a trusty. Worked right here in our records section for a while. Have a seat. I guess we'll be getting him back now." Armijo indicated a gray steel chair with a gray plastic cushion. "Violated his parole, is that it?"

"Looks like it," Chee said. "I guess you could say he's a suspect in a burglary. Anyway, we need to know more about him."

"Here he is." Armijo handed Chee a brown cardboard accordion file. "All about Joseph Musket."

Chee put the file on his lap. He'd read through such files before. He knew what was in them, and what wasn't. "You said you knew him," Chee said. "What was he like?"

"Like?" The question surprised Armijo. He looked puzzled. He shrugged. "Well, you know. Quiet. Didn't say much. Did his work." Armijo frowned. "What do you mean, what was he like?"

A good question, Chee thought. What did he mean? What was he looking for? "Did he tell jokes?" Chee asked. "Was he the kind of guy who sort of takes over a job, or did you have to tell him everything? Have any friends? That sort of thing."

"I don't know," Armijo said. His expression said he wished he hadn't started the conversation. "I'd tell him what to do and he'd do it. Didn't ever say much. Quiet. He was an Indian." Armijo glanced at Chee to see if that explained

115

it. Then he went on, explaining the job—how Musket would come in each afternoon, how he'd set up the files on the new prisoners received that day and then sort through the File basket and add whatever new material might have developed to the folders of other inmates. "Not a very demanding job," Armijo said. "But he did it well enough. Didn't make mistakes. Got good reports."

"How about friends?" Chee asked.

"Oh, he had friends," Armijo said. "In here, you got money, you got friends."

"Musket had money?" That surprised Chee.

"In his canteen account," Armijo said. "That's all you can have. No cash, of course. Just credit for smokes, candy, and stuff like that. All the little extras."

"You mean more money than he could earn in here? Outside money?"

"He had connections," Armijo said. "Lots of narcotics dealers have connections. Some lawyer depositing money into their account."

And that seemed to be all Armijo knew. He showed Chee into an adjoining room and left him with the file.

In the file there were first the photographs.

Joseph Musket stared out at Chee: an oval face, clean shaven, a line extending down the center of the forehead, the expression blank—the face a man puts on when he has cleared everything out of his mind except the need to endure. He hadn't changed a lot, Chee thought, beyond the change caused by the thin mustache, a few added pounds, and a few added years. But then maybe he had changed. Chee turned his eyes away from the stolid eyes of Musket and looked at his profile. That was all he had seen of Joseph Musket—a quick disinterested glance at a stranger walking past. The profile showed Chee a high, straight forehead— the look of intelligence. Nothing more.

He looked away from the face and noted the vital statistics.

116

Musket today would be in his early thirties, he noticed, which was about what he had guessed. The rest checked out with what he had already learned from Musket's probation officer: born near Mexican Water, son of Simon Musket and Fannie Tsossie, educated at Teec Nos Pos boarding school and the high school at Cottonwood. As he'd remembered from what the probation officer had shown him at Flagstaff, Musket was doing three-to-five for possession of narcotics with intent to sell.

Chee read more carefully. Musket's police record was unremarkable. His first rap had been at eighteen in Gallup, drunk and disorderly. Then had come an arrest in Albuquerque for grand theft, dismissed, and another Albuquerque arrest for burglary, which had led to a two-year sentence and referral to a drug treatment program, suspended. Another burglary charge, this one in El Paso, had led to a one-to-three sentence in Huntsville; and then came what Chee had been (at least subconsciously) looking for—Joe Musket's graduation into the more lethal level of crime. It had been an armed robbery of a Seven-Eleven Store at Las Cruces, New Mexico. On this one, the grand jury hadn't indicted, and the charge had been dismissed. Chee sorted through the pages, looking for the investigating officer's report. It sounded typical. Two men, one outside in a car, the other inside looking at the magazines until the last customer leaves, then the gun shown to the clerk, money from the register stuffed into a grocery bag, the clerk locked in the storeroom, and two suspects arrested after abandoning the getaway car. Musket had been found hiding between garbage containers in an alley, but the clerk wasn't ready to swear he was the man he'd seen waiting in the car outside. At the bottom of the page, a Xerox out of the Las Cruces police files, was a handwritten note. It said:

"True bill on West—no bill on Musket."

Chee glanced quickly back up the page, found the suspect-identification line. The man who'd gone into the store with the gun while Joseph Musket waited in the car was identified as Thomas Rodney West, age 30, address, Ideal Motel, 2929 Railroad Avenue, El Paso.

It didn't really surprise Chee. West had said Musket was a friend of his son's. That was the reason he'd given Musket the job. And West had said his son had bad friends and had been in trouble, and had been killed. But how had he been killed? Chee hurried now. He found Thomas Rodney West once again in the investigation report which covered the drug bust that had sent Musket to the Santa Fe prison. He had been nailed along with Musket in the pickup truck carrying eight hundred pounds of marijuana. The pot had been unloaded off a light aircraft in the desert south of Alamogordo, New Mexico. The plane had eluded the DEA trap, the pickup hadn't. Chee put down the Musket file and stared for a long moment at the gray concrete wall. Then he went into Armijo's office. Armijo looked up from his paperwork, teeth white.

"Do you keep files on inmates after they're dead?"

"Sure." Armijo's smile widened. "In the dead file."

"I'm not sure he was here," Chee said. "Fellow named Thomas Rodney West."

Armijo's smile lost its luster. "He was here," he said. "Got killed."

"In here?"

"This year," Armijo said. "In the recreation yard." He got up and was stooping to pull open the bottom drawer of a filing cabinet. "Things like that happen now and then," he said.

"Somebody?" Chee said. "It wasn't solved?"

"No," Armijo said. "Five hundred men all around him and nobody saw a thing. That's the way it works, usually."

The accordion file of Thomas Rodney West was identical to that of Joseph Musket (a.k.a. Ironfingers Musket), except that the string which secured its flap was tied with a knot, giving it the finality of death, instead of a bow, which suggested the impermanence of parole. Chee carried it back into the waiting room, put it beside the Musket file, and worked the knot loose with his fingernails.

Here there was no question of recognizing the mug shots that looked glumly out from the identification sheet. Thomas Rodney West, convict, looked just like Tom West, schoolboy, and Tom West, Marine, whose face Chee had studied in the photographs in the Burnt Water Trading Post. He also looked a lot like his father. The expression had the suffering blankness that police photographers and the circumstances impose on such shots. But behind that, there was the heavy strength and the same forcefulness that marked the face of the older West. Chee noticed that West had been born the same month as Musket, West was nine days younger. Chee corrected the thought. The knife in the recreation yard had changed that, sparing young West the aging process. Now Musket was a month or so older.

Chee worked through the pages, wondering what he was looking for. He noticed that West had come out of the armed robbery with a plea bargain deal: Guilty with a four-year sentence, suspended into probation. He'd still been on probation when the narcotics arrest happened. And he was carrying a gun when arrested. (Musket hadn't been, Chee recalled. Had he been smart enough to ditch it when he saw what was happening?) Those two factors had netted West a stiffer, five-to-seven-year rap.

It was warm in the room, and airless. Chee flipped to the last page and read the data on the death of Thomas Rodney West. It was as Armijo had reported. At 11:17 A.M., July 6, the guard in tower 7 had noticed a body in the dust of the recreation yard. No inmate was near it. He called down to the guard in the yard. West was found to be unconscious, dying from three deep puncture wounds. Subsequent

119

interrogation of inmates revealed no one who had seen what had happened. Subsequent search of the yard had produced a sharpened screwdriver and a wood rasp which had been converted into makeshift daggers. Both were stained with blood that matched West's blood type. Next of kin, Jacob West, Burnt Water, Arizona, had been notified and had claimed the body on July 8. The carbon copy of an autopsy report was the final page in the file. It showed that Thomsas Rodney West, his first name mutilated by a typographical error, had died of a slashed aortal artery and two wounds to his abdominal cavity.

Chee flipped back a page and looked at the date. A busy month, July. West had been stabbed to death July 6. John Doe had been killed July 10, almost certainly, since his body was found early on the morning of July 11. On July 28 Joseph Musket disappeared after burglarizing the Burnt Water store. Any connection? Chee could think of none. But there might be, if he could identify Doe. He yawned. Up early this morning, and little sleep during the night. He lit a cigaret. He'd read quickly again through everything in the West file, and then return to the Musket file and finish it, and get out of there. The place oppressed him. Made him uneasy. Made him feel an odd, unusual sense of sorrow.

There was nothing unusual in West's commissary credit account, or in his health check reports, or in his correspondence log, which included only his father, a woman in El Paso, and an El Paso attorney. Then Chee turned to the log of visitors.

On July 2, four days before he'd been stabbed to death, Thomas Rodney West had been visited by T. L. Johnson, agent, U.S. Drug Enforcement Agency. Purpose: Official business. Chee stared at the entry, and then at the ones which preceded it. West had been visited five times since his arrival at the prison. By his father, and once by the woman from El Paso, and twice by someone who had identified himself as Jerald R. Jansen, attorney at law, Petroleum Towers Bldg, Houston, Texas.

"Ah." Chee said it aloud. He sat back in the chair and stared at the ceiling. Jansen. Attorney. Houston. He'd met Jansen. Jansen dead. Sitting cold and silent beside the basalt, holding the Hopi Cultural Center message between thumb and finger. Chee blew a plume of smoke at the ceiling, rocked the chair forward, and checked the dates. Jansen had visited West on February 17, and again on May 2. Long before the parole of Joseph Musket, and then after it. Then West had been visited by the DEA's freckled, red-haired T. L. Johnson four days before he'd been stabbed. Chee thought about that for a moment, looking for meaning. He found nothing but a take-your-choice set of contradictory possibilities.

Then he checked Joseph Musket's log of visitors. He'd had none. Not one visitor in more than two years in prison. He checked Musket's log of correspondents. None. No letters in. No letters out. The isolated man. Chee closed the Musket file and put it atop the West file.

Armijo was no longer alone. Two convicts were at work in his office now—a burr-haired young blond who glanced up from his typewriter as Chee brought the files in and then looked quickly back at his work, and a middle-aged black man with a gauze bandage on the back of his neck. The black man seemed to be Musket's replacement as file clerk. He was sifting papers into files, eyeing Chee curiously.

"If West had any close friends in here, I'd sure like to talk to one of them," Chee said. "What do you think?"

"I don't know," Armijo said. "I don't know anything about friends."

How would he know? Chee thought. Such things as friendships were not the stuff that filled accordion files.

"Any way of finding out?" Chee asked. "Down the grapevine, or whatever you do?"

Armijo looked doubtful.

"Who's in charge of inside security?" Chee asked.

"That would be the deputy warden," Armijo said. "I'll call him."

While Armijo dialed, the sound of the burr head's typewriter resumed. Typing makes it hard for him to listen, Chee thought.

The deputy warden for security wanted to talk to Chee directly, and then he wanted to know what Chee was doing in the prison, and why, specifically, he wanted to talk to a friend of West.

"Nothing to do with anything in here," Chee assured him. "We've got an unsolved burglary on the reservation, and we're looking for a parole violator named Musket. Musket got sent up with West. They were friends from way back. Did an armed robbery or so together before going into drugs. I just need to know if West and Musket stayed friendly in prison. Things like that."

The deputy warden said nothing for several seconds. Then he told Chee to wait, he'd call back.

Chee waited almost an hour. Burr head typed, eyeing him now and then. The black man with the bandaged neck finished emptying the Out basket into the proper accordion files and left. Armijo had explained that he was working on his annual report, which was late. He used a pocket calculator, comparing figures and compiling some sort of list. Chee sat in his gray metal chair, thinking now and then, and now and then listening to the sounds that came through the door beside his right ear. Footsteps, approaching and receding, an occasional distant metallic sound, once an echoing clang, once a whistle, shrill and brief. Never a voice, never a spoken word. Why did Johnson visit Thomas Rodney West? Had West heard of the impending drug delivery near Burnt Water and summoned the agent to trade information for a parole recommendation? West must have been connected to the group involved in the transfer. Why else had Jansen visited him twice? Johnson could have known that. Probably would have. Almost certainly did. Obviously did. Had he visited, hoping to pry out of West some information about the impending shipment? That seemed the best bet.

The sound now was the telephone shrilling. Armijo spoke into it, listened. Handed it to Chee.

"Fellow will talk to you," the deputy warden said. "Name's Archer. Good friend of West. Very good." The deputy warden laughed. "If you know what I mean."

"Girl friend?" Chee asked.

"I think it was boy friend," the D.W. said.

The same middle-aged Chicano appeared, to guide Chee, taking him down a long, blank corridor. The two convicts they met on the journey walked against the walls, giving them the middle of the aisle. The interview room was windowless and the fluorescent tubes which lit it gave its dirty white paint a grayish tinge. The man named Archer was big, perhaps forty years old, with the body of a man who worked on the weights. His nose had been broken a long time ago and broken again more recently and the scars from one of the breaks glistened white against the pallor of his skin. Archer was sitting behind the counter that split the small room, looking curiously at Chee through a pane of glass. A guard leaned against the wall behind him, smoking.

"My name's Jim Chee," Chee said to Archer. "I know Tom West's father. I need a little information. Just a little."

"This can be a short conversation," Archer said. "I wasn't in the yard when it happened. I don't know a damned thing."

"That's not what I'm asking about," Chee said. "I want to know why he wanted to talk to T. L. Johnson."

Archer looked blank.

"Why he wanted to talk to Johnson the narcotics agent."

Archer's face flushed. "T. L. Johnson," he said slowly, memorizing the name. "Was that who it was? Tom didn't want to talk to that son of a bitch. He didn't know nothing to tell him. He was scared to death of it." Archer snorted. "For a damn good reason. The son of a bitch set him up."

"It wasn't West's idea, then?"

"Hell, no, it wasn't. Nobody in here is going to volunteer to talk to a narc. Not in here, they're not. The bastard set him up. You know what he did? He arranged to take him out of here. Right down the front walk, right out the front gate, right into his car, and drive away. Just drove down toward Cerrillos, out of sight of the prison, and sat there. No way for West to prove he hadn't snitched." Archer glared at Chee, his pallid face still flushed. "Dirty son of a bitch," he said.

"How do you know about this?" Chee asked.

"When they brought him back, Tom told me." Archer shook his head. "He was mad and he was scared. He said the narc wanted to know about when a shipment was going to come in, and where, and all about it, and when Tom told him he didn't know nothing, Johnson laughed at him and just parked out there and said he was going to stay parked until all the cons figured he had time to spill his guts."

"Scared," Chee asked. "Was he? He didn't ask to get put in segregation, where he'd be safe. Or if he did ask, it wasn't in the files."

"He talked about it," Archer said. "But once you go in there you got to stay. That's rat country. Everybody in there is a snitch. You go in there you can't come out."

"So he decided to risk it?"

"Yeah," Archer said. "He had a lot of respect in here. So do I." He looked at Chee, his expression strained. "It seemed like we could risk it," he said. "It seemed like a good gamble."

Archer had argued for the gamble, Chee guessed. Now he wanted Chee to understand it.

"Can you tell me anything about who killed him, or why, or anything?"

Archer's face assumed the same expression Chee had always noticed in official police identification photographs.

"I don't have no ideas about that," he said. "Look, I've got to get out of here. Work to do."

"One more thing," Chee said. "He got sent up here with a man named Joseph Musket. Friends from way back. Did they stay friends?"

"Musket's out," Archer said. "Paroled."

"But were they friends up until then?"

Archer looked thoughtful. Chee guessed he was looking for traps. Apparently he found none.

"They were friends," Archer said. He shook his head, and his face relaxed. "Really," he said, "Tom was a great guy. He had a lot of respect in here. People didn't screw with him. The bad ones, you know, they'd walk around him. He looked after Musket some, I think." Then Archer's expression changed. "Maybe I said that wrong. Tom was Musket's friend, but I don't know if it really worked both ways. I didn't never trust Musket. He was one of them guys, you know, who you never know about." Archer got up. "Just too damn smart. Just too damn clever. You know what I mean?"

On his way out, Chee stopped at Armijo's office a final time to use the telephone. He dialed the deputy warden's number.

"I wonder if I could get you to check and see if a DEA agent named T. L. Johnson asked permission to take Thomas West out of the prison," Chee asked. "Was that arranged?"

The deputy warden didn't have to look it up. "Yeah," he said. "He did that. Sometimes we let that happen when there's a good reason for privacy."

20

◆

Chee took the roundabout way home—circling north through Santa Fe and Chama instead of southward down the Rio Grande valley through Albuquerque. He took the northern route because it led through beautiful country. He planned to play the tapes he had made of Frank Sam Nakai singing the Night Chant and thereby memorize another section of that complicated eight-day ritual. Beauty helped put him in the mood for the sort of concentration required. Now it didn't work. His mind kept turning to the distraction of unresolved questions. Ironfingers? "Too damn clever," Archer had called him, but not too smart to give stolen jewelry to a girl. Had Johnson, as it seemed, deliberately set up Thomas Rodney West for a prison yard killing? And if he had, why? Who had taken the body of Palanzer from the carryall? And why had the body been left there, in its cocoon of Lysol mist, in the first place? The moon rose over the jagged ridge of the Sangre de Cristo range as he drove up the Chama valley. It hung in the clear, dark sky like a great luminous rock, flooding the landscape with light. When he reached Abiquiu village, he pulled off at the Standard station, bought gas, and used the pay phone. He called Cowboy Dashee's home number. The phone rang six times before Cowboy answered. Dashee had been asleep.

"I didn't think bachelors went to bed so early," Chee said. "Sorry about that. But I need to know something. Did they find the dope?"

126

"Hell," Dashee said. "We didn't find nothing. That's why I'm trying to get some sleep. The sheriff wanted us out there at daylight. Everybody figured they'd hauled that stuff up the arroyo in that carryall and then hid it someplace around there. If they did, we sure as hell couldn't find it."

"Does anybody really know what you're looking for?" Chee asked. "Any idea how big it is, or what it weighs, or how big a hole it would take to bury it?"

"Seem to," Cowboy said. "They were talking about a hundred pounds or so and something as bulky as maybe three forty-pound sacks of flour. Or maybe a bunch of smaller packages."

"So they do know what they're after," Chee said. "The DEA was there?"

"Johnson was. And a couple of FBI agents from Flagstaff."

"And you didn't find anything interesting? No dope, no machine guns, no tape-recorded messages on how to ransom the cargo, no dead bodies, no maps. Absolutely nothing?"

"Found a few tracks," Cowboy said. "Nothing useful. There just flat wasn't any big cache of dope hidden up there. If they hauled it up there in that GMC in the first place, then they just hauled it off again, and we didn't see any sign of that. Wouldn't make sense anyway. Think about it. No sense to it."

Chee did think about it. He thought about it intermittently all the way north to Chama and then on the long westward drive across the sprawling Jicarilla Apache reservation. As Cowboy said, there was no sense to it. Another apparently irrational knot to be unraveled. Chee could think of only one possible place to find an end to the string. Whoever was vandalizing Windmill Number 6 had been a hidden witness at the crash. He must have seen something. It was merely a matter of finding him.

It was afternoon when Chee returned to the windmill. He stood looking at it, realizing that any sensible, sensitive human could come to detest it. It was an awkward discordant shape. It clashed with the gentle slope on which it stood. The sun reflected painfully bright from the zinc coating which armored it against softening rust. It made ugly clanking, groaning noises in the breeze. The last time he'd been here his mood had been cheerful as the morning, and then the mill had seemed merely neutral—a harmless object. But today heat shimmered off the drought-stricken landscape and dust moved in the arid wind, and his mood was as negative as the weather. This ugly object represented injustice to thousands of Navajos. Any one of them might be vandalizing it, or all of them, or any member of their multitudinous families. Or maybe they were taking turns vandalizing it. Whatever, he didn't blame them and he'd never solve the mystery. Maybe it wasn't a Navajo at all. Maybe it was some artistic Hopi whose sense of aesthetics was offended.

Chee walked past the steel storage tank and peered into it. Bone dry. A reservoir for dust. Leaning against the hot metal, Chee took inventory of what he knew. It was all negative. The vandal always used some simple means—no dynamite, cutting torches, or machinery. In other words, nothing to trace down. He apparently arrived on foot or by horse, since Chee had never found any wheel tracks which he couldn't account for. And Jake West had guessed it wasn't a local Navajo, for what that was worth. West could be misleading him deliberately to protect a friend, or West could be wrong. West had not, however, been wrong about BIA efficiency. The BIA crew had apparently brought the wrong parts, or done something wrong. The gearbox was still not operating and the mill's creaks and groans were as impotent as they'd been for most of the summer.

Chee repeated his methodical examination of the grounds, working in widening circles. He found no off-brand cigarets smeared with odd-colored lipstick, no discarded screwdrivers with handles which still might retain fingerprints, no

lost billfolds containing driver's licenses with color photographs of the windmill vandal, no footprints, no tire tracks,
nothing. He hadn't expected to. He sat down on the slope,
cupped his hand against the dusty wind, and managed to
get a cigaret lit. He stared down toward the mill, frowning.
He hadn't found anything specific, but something in his subconscious was teasing him. Had he found something without
realizing it? Exactly what had he found? Almost nothing.
Even the rabbit droppings and the trails of the kangaroo
rats were old. The little desert rodents which congregate
wherever there is water had moved away. Last year the
inevitable leakage around the windmill had provided for
them. But now the thick growth of sunflowers, tumbleweeds,
and desert asters which had flourished around the storage
tank were just dead stalks. The plants were dead and the
rodents were gone because the vandal had dried up their
chance of living here. Desert ecology had clicked back into
balance on this hillside. The rodents would have returned
to the arroyo with its seeping spring, with its *pahos* and
its guardian spirit, Chee guessed, but the spring, too, was
virtually dry. The victim of drought. Or was it?

Chee jumped to his feet, snubbed out his cigaret, and
hurried down the slope toward the arroyo. He trotted along
the sandy bottom, following the path the moccasins of the
shrine's guardian had made. The shrine looked just as he
had left it. He crouched under the shale overhang, careful
not to disturb the *pahos*. When he had been here before,
there had been a film of water on the granite under the
shale, so shallow that it was not much more than a pattern
of wetness. Chee studied the rock surface. The dampness
had spread. Not much, but it had spread. The spring had
been barely alive when he had seen it before. It was still
barely alive. But the spring was no longer dying.

Chee walked back to his pickup truck, climbed in, and
drove away without a backward glance. He was finished

with the windmill. It offered no more mysteries. He'd stop at the Burnt Water store and call Cowboy Dashee. He'd tell Cowboy he had to talk to the keeper of the shrine. Cowboy wouldn't like it. But Cowboy would find him.

21

Cowboy had arranged to meet him at the junction of Arizona Highway 87 and Navajo Route 3. "We're going to have to go to Piutki," Cowboy had told him. "That's where he lives. But I don't want to have you floundering around up there by yourself, getting lost. So meet me, and I'll take you up."

"About when?"

"About seven," Cowboy said.

So Chee had arrived about seven. Five minutes before, to be exact. He stood beside his pickup truck, stretching his muscles. The early evening sun lit the slopes of Second Mesa behind him, making a glittering reflection off the hot asphalt of Navajo 3 where it zigzagged upward. Just to the north, the cliff of First Mesa was dappled with shadow. Chee himself stood in the shadow. A cloud which had been building slowly all afternoon over the San Francisco Peaks had broken free of the mountain's updrafts and was drifting eastward. It was still at least twenty miles to the west, but its crest had built high enough now to block out the slanting light of sun. The heat of the day had produced other such thunderheads. Three, in an irregular row, were sailing across the Painted Desert between Chee and Winslow. One, Chee noticed with pleasure, was actually dragging a small tail of rain across Tovar Mesa. But none of the smaller clouds promised much. With sundown they would quickly evaporate in the arid sky. The cloud spawned by the San Francisco Peaks

131

was another matter. It was huge, its top pushed up into the stratospheric cold by its internal winds, and its lower levels blue-black with the promise of rain. As Chee appraised it, he heard the mutter of thunder. The clouds would be visible for a hundred miles in every direction, from Navajo Mountain across the Utah border, as far east as the Chuska Range in New Mexico. One cloud wouldn't break a drought, but it takes one cloud to start the process. For a thousand Navajo sheepmen across this immense dry tableland the cloud meant hope that rain, running arroyos, and new grass would again be part of the *hozro* of their lives. To the Hopis, rain would mean more than that. It would mean the endorsement of the supernatural. The Hopis had called for the clouds, and the clouds had come. It would mean that after a year of blighted dust, things were right again between the Peaceful People of the Hopi Mesas and their kachina spirits.

Chee leaned against the truck, enjoying the cool, damp breeze which the cloud was now producing, enjoying the contrast between the dappled browns and tans of the First Mesa cliffs and the dark-blue sky over them. Above him the rim of the cliff was not cliff at all, but the stone walls of the houses of Walpi. From here it was hard to believe that. The tiny windows seemed to be holes in the living rock of the mesa.

Chee glanced at his watch. Cowboy was late. He retrieved his notebook from the front seat, and turned to a clean page. Across the top he wrote: "Questions and Answers." Then he wrote: "1. Where is J. Musket? Did Musket kill John Doe? Witch? Crazy? Tied up with the narcotics heist?" He drew a line down the center of the page, separating the Answers section. Here he wrote: "1. Evidence he away from work day Doe killed. Musket connected with narcotics. Likely came to Burnt Water to set up delivery. How else? Would have known the country well enough to hide the GMC."

Chee studied the entries. He tapped a front tooth with the butt of the ballpoint pen. He wrote under Questions: "Why the burglary? To provide a logical reason for disappearing from the trading post?" Chee frowned at that, and wrote: "What happened to the stolen jewelry?" He drew a line under that all the way across the page. Under it he wrote:

"Who is John Doe? Somebody from the narcotics business? Working with Musket? Did Musket kill him because Doe smelled the double cross? Did Musket make it look like a witch killing to confuse things?" No answers here. Just questions. He drew another horizontal line and wrote under it:

"Where's Palanzer's body? Why hide it in the GMC? To confuse those looking for dope? Why take it out of the GMC? Because someone knew I'd found it? Who knew? The man who walked up the arroyo in the dark? Musket? Dashee?" He stared at the name, feeling disloyal. But Dashee knew. He'd told Dashee where to find the truck. And Dashee could have been at the windmill site when the crash happened. He wondered if he could learn where Dashee had been the night John Doe's body had been hidden. And then he shook his head and drew a line through "Dashee," and then another line. Under that he wrote a single word: "Witch."

Under that he wrote: "Any reason to connect witch killing with dope?" He stared at the question, worrying his lower lip between his teeth. Then he wrote: "Coincidence of time and place." He paused a moment, then jotted beside it: "Doe died July 10, West died July 6." He was still thinking about that when Dashee drove up.

"Right on the money," Cowboy said.

"You're late," Chee said.

"Operating on Navajo time," Cowboy said. "Seven means sometime tonight. Let's take my car."

Chee got in.

"You ever been to Piutki?"

"I don't think so," Chee said. "Where is it?"

133

"Up on First Mesa," Cowboy said. "Back behind Hano on the ridge." Cowboy was driving more sedately than usual. He rolled the patrol car down Navajo Route 3 and did a left turn onto the narrower asphalt which made the steep, winding climb up the face of the mesa. His face was still, thoughtful.

Worried, Chee thought. We're getting involved in something religious.

"There's not much left of Piutki," Cowboy said. "It's pretty well abandoned. Used to be the village of the Fog Clan with some Bow Clan, and the Fog Clan is just about extinct. Not many Bow left either."

Fog Clan touched a memory. Chee tried to recall what he'd learned about Hopi ethnology in his anthro classes at the University of New Mexico, and what he'd read since, and what he'd picked up from gossip. The Fog Clan had brought to the Hopis the gift of sorcery. That had been its ceremonial contribution to Hopi society. And of course, the sorcerers were the *powaqas*, the "two-hearts," the Hopi culture's peculiar version of what witches were like. There was something about the Bow Clan, too. What? Chee's reliable memory served up the answer. He'd read it in some treatise on Hopi clan history. When the Bow Clan had completed its great migrations and arrived at the Hopi Mesas, it had accumulated such a reputation for creating trouble that the Bear Clan elders had repeatedly refused its request for lands and a village home. And after it had finally been allowed to join the other clans, the Bows had been involved in the single bloody incident in the history of the Peaceful People. When the Arrowshaft Clan at Awatovi had allowed Spanish priests to move into the village, the Bows had suggested a punitive attack. The Arrowshaft males had been slaughtered in their kivas, and the women and children had been scattered among the other villages. The Arrowshaft clan had not survived.

"This man we're going to see," Chee said. "What's his clan?"

Cowboy eyed him. "Why you ask that?"

"You said it was the Fog Clan village. I heard somewhere that the Fog Clan had died out."

"More or less," Cowboy said. "But the Hopis use a sort of linked clan system, and the Fog is linked to the Cloud Clan and the Water Clan and . . ." Cowboy let it trail away. He shifted into second gear for the steep climb along the mesa cliff.

The road reached the saddle of the narrow ridge. It climbed straight ahead to Walpi. Cowboy jerked the patrol car into the narrow turn up the other side of the saddle toward Sichomovi and Hano. The rear wheels skidded. Cowboy muttered something under his breath.

Chee had been watching him. "Had a bad day?"

Cowboy said nothing. Clearly Cowboy had had a bad day.

"What's bothering you?" Chee asked.

Cowboy laughed. But he didn't sound amused. "Nothing," he said.

"You'd just as soon not be doing this?"

Cowboy shrugged.

The patrol car edged past the ancient stone walls of Sichomovi . . . or was it Hano now? Chee wasn't sure yet where one of the villages ended and the other began. It seemed inconceivable to Chee that the Hopis had chosen to live like this—collecting right on top of each other in these tight little towns without privacy or breathing room. His own people had done exactly the opposite. Laws of nature, he thought. Hopis collect, Navajos scatter. But what was bothering Cowboy? He thought about it.

"Who is this guy we're going to see?"

"His name is Taylor Sawkatewa," Cowboy said. "And I think we're wasting our time."

"Don't think he'll tell us anything?"

"Why should he?" Cowboy said. The tone was curt, and Cowboy seemed to realize it. When he continued, there was a hint of apology in his tone. "He's about a million years old. More traditional than the worst traditional. On top of that, I hear he's sort of crazy."

And, Chee thought, you hear he's a *powaqa*. And that's what's making you a little edgy. Chee thought about what he'd heard about *powaqas*. It made him a little edgy, too.

"Not much use appealing to his duty as a law-abiding citizen, I guess," Chee said.

Cowboy laughed. "I don't think so. Be like trying to explain to a Brahma bull why he should hold still while you're putting a surcingle around him."

They were clear of Hano now, jolting down a stony track which followed the mesa rim. The cloud loomed in the southwest. The sun on the horizon lit the underface of its great anvil top a glittering white, but at its lower level its color varied. A thousand gradations of gray from almost white to almost black, and—from the dying sun—shades of rose and pink and red. To Cowboy Dashee's people such a cloud would have sacred symbolism. To Chee's people, it was simply beautiful, and thus valuable just for itself.

"Another thing," Cowboy said. "Old Sawkatewa don't speak English. That's what they tell me anyway. So I'll have to interpret."

"Anything else I need to know about him?"

Cowboy shrugged.

"You didn't tell me what his clan is."

Cowboy slowed the patrol car, eased it past a jagged rock and over a rut. "He's Fog," he said.

"So the Fog Clan isn't extinct?"

"Really, it is," Cowboy said. "Hardly any left. All their ceremonial duties—what's left—they're owned by the Water Clan now, or Cloud Clan. It was that way even when I was a boy. Long before that, I guess. My daddy said the last time the Ya Ya Society did anything was when he was a little boy—and I don't think that was a full ceremony. Walpi kicked them out a long time ago."

"Kicked them out?"

"The Ya Ya Society," Cowboy said. He didn't offer to expand. From what Chee could remember hearing about the society, it controlled initiation into the various levels of sorcery. In other words, it was a sensitive subject and Cowboy didn't want to talk about it to a non-Hopi.

"Why did they kick 'em out?" Chee asked.

"Caused trouble," Cowboy said.

"Isn't that the society that used to initiate people who wanted to become two-hearts?"

"Yeah," Cowboy said.

"I remember somebody telling me something about it," Chee said. "Somebody told me they deal where they saw a pine tree trunk on the ground and the sorcerer caused it to move up and down in the air."

Cowboy said nothing.

"That's right?" Chee asked. "A lot of magic at a Ya Ya ceremony."

"But if you have power, and you use it for the wrong reasons, then you lose the power," Cowboy said. "That's what we're told."

"This man we're going to see," Chee said. "He was a member of the Ya Ya Society. That right?"

Cowboy eased the patrol car over another rough spot. The sun was down now, the horizon a streak of fire. The cloud was closer and beginning to drop a screen of rain. It evaporated at least a thousand feet above ground level, but it provided a translucent screen which filtered the reddish light.

"I heard he was a member of the Ya Ya," Cowboy said. "You can hear just about anything."

The village of Piutki had never had the size or importance

of such places as Oraibi, or Walpi, or even Shongopovi. At its peak it had housed only part of the small Bow Clan, and the even smaller Fog Clan. That peak had passed long ago, probably in the eighteenth or nineteenth century. Now many of its houses had been abandoned. Their roofs had fallen in and their walls had been quarried for stone to maintain houses still occupied. The great cloud now dominated the sky, and illuminated the old place with a red twilight. The breeze followed the patrol car with outriders of dust. Cowboy flicked on the headlights.

"Place looks empty," Chee said.

"It almost is," Cowboy agreed.

The plaza was small, houses on two sides of it in ruins. Chee noticed that the kiva, too, was in disrepair. The steps that led to its roof were rotted and broken, and the ladder that should have protruded from its rooftop entrance was missing. It was a small kiva, and low, its walls rising only some five feet above the dusty plaza earth. It seemed as dead as the men who had built it so long ago.

"Well," Cowboy said. "Here we are." He stopped the car beside the kiva. Beyond it, one of the houses that still walled two sides of the plaza was occupied. The breeze blew smoke from its chimney toward them, and a small pile of coal stood beside its doorway. The door opened. A boy—perhaps ten or twelve—looked out at them. The boy was an albino.

Cowboy left the car unlocked and walked through the blowing dust without waiting for Chee. He spoke to the boy at the door in Hopi, listened to his answer, thought about it, and spoke again. The boy disappeared inside.

"He said Sawkatewa is working. He'd tell him he had visitors," Cowboy said.

Chee nodded. He heard a thumping of thunder and glanced up at the cloud. Only its upper levels were red with sunset now. Below that, its color shaded from blue to almost black. While he looked at it, the black flashed with yellow, and flashed again. Internal lightning was illuminating it. They waited. Dust eddied in the plaza. The air was much cooler now. It smelled of rain. The sound of thunder reached them. This time it boomed, and boomed again.

The boy reappeared. He looked at Chee through thick-lensed glasses and then at Cowboy, and spoke in Hopi.

"In we go," Cowboy said.

Taylor Sawkatewa was sitting on a small metal chair, winding yarn onto a spindle. He was looking at them, his bright black eyes curious. But his hands never stopped their quick, agile work. He spoke to Cowboy, and motioned toward a green plastic sofa which stood against the entrance wall, and then he examined Chee. He smiled and nodded.

"He says sit down," Cowboy said.

They sat on the green plastic. It was a small room, a little off square, the walls flaking whitewash. A kerosene lamp, its glass chimney sooty, cast a wavering yellow light.

Sawkatewa spoke to both of them, smiling at Chee again. Chee smiled back.

Then Cowboy spoke at length. The old man listened. His hands worked steadily, moving the gray-white wool from a skein in a cardboard beer carton beside his chair onto the long wooden spindle. His eyes left Cowboy and settled on Chee's face. He was a very old man, far beyond the point where curiosity can be interpreted as rudeness. Navajos, too, sometimes live to be very old and Chee's Slow Talking Dinee had its share of them.

Cowboy completed his statement, paused, added a brief postscript, then turned to Chee.

"I told him I would now tell you what I'd told him," Cowboy said. "And what I told him was who you are and that we are here because we are trying to find out something about the plane crash out in Wepo Wash."

"I think you should tell him what happened in a lot of detail," Chee said. "Tell him that two men were killed in the airplane, and that two other men have been killed because of what the airplane carried. And tell him that it would help us a lot if someone had been there and had seen what happened and could tell us what he saw." Chee kept his eyes on Sawkatewa as he said this. The old man was listening intently, smiling slightly. He understands a little English, Chee decided. Maybe he understands more than a little.

Cowboy spoke in Hopi. Sawkatewa listened. He had the round head and the broad fine nose of many Hopis, and a long jaw, made longer by his toothlessness. His cheeks and his chin wrinkled around his sunken mouth, but his skin, like his eyes, looked ageless and his hair, cut in the bangs of the traditional Hopi male, was still mostly black. While he listened, his fingers worked the yarn, limber as eels.

Cowboy finished his translation. The old man waited a polite moment, and then he spoke to Cowboy in rapid Hopi, finished speaking, and laughed.

Cowboy made a gesture of denial. Sawkatewa spoke again, laughed again. Cowboy responded at length in Hopi. Then he looked at Chee.

"He says you must think that he is old and foolish. He says that he has heard that somebody is breaking the windmill out there and that we are looking for the one who broke it to put him in jail. He says that you wish to trick him into saying that he was by the windmill on that night."

"What did you tell him?" Chee asked.

"I denied it."

"But how?" Chee asked. "Tell me everything you told him."

Cowboy frowned. "I told him we didn't think he broke the windmill. I said we thought some Navajos broke it because they were angry at having to leave Hopi land."

"Please tell Taylor Sawkatewa that we wish to withdraw that denial," Chee said, looking directly into Sawkatewa's eyes as he said it. "Tell him that we do not deny that we think he might be the man who broke the windmill."

"Man," Cowboy said. "You're crazy. What are you driving at?"

"Tell him," Chee said.

Cowboy shrugged. He spoke to Sawkatewa in Hopi. Sawkatewa looked surprised, and interested. For the first time his fingers left off their nimble work. Sawkatewa folded his hands in his lap. He turned and spoke into the darkness of the adjoining room, where the albino boy was standing.

"What did he say?" Chee asked.

"He told the boy to make us some coffee," Cowboy said.

"Now tell him that I am studying to be a *yataalii* among my people and that I study under an old man, a man who like himself is a hosteen much respected by his people. Tell him that this old uncle of mine has taught me respect for the power of the Hopis and for all that they have been taught by their Holy People about bringing the rain and keeping the world from being destroyed. Tell him that when I was a child I would come with my uncle to First Mesa so that our prayers could be joined with those of the Hopis at the ceremonials. Tell him that."

Cowboy put it into Hopi. Sawkatewa listened, his eyes shifting from Cowboy to Chee. He sat motionless. Then he nodded.

"Tell him that my uncle taught me that in many ways the Dinee and the Hopi are very, very different. We are taught by our Holy People, by Changing Woman, and by the Talking God how we must live and the things we must do to keep ourselves in beauty with the world around us. But we were not taught how to call the rain clouds. We cannot draw the blessing of water out of the sky as the Hopis have been taught to do. We do not have this great power that the Hopis were given and we respect the Hopis for it and honor them."

Cowboy repeated it. The sound of thunder came through

the roof, close now. A sharp, cracking explosion followed by rumbling echoes. Good timing, Chee thought. The old man nodded again.

"My uncle told me that the Hopis have power because they were taught a way to do things, but they will lose that power if they do them wrong." Chee continued: "That is why we say we do not know whether a Hopi or a Navajo is breaking the windmill. A Navajo might do it because he was angry." Chee paused, raised a hand slightly, palm forward, making sure that the old man noticed the emphasis. "But a Hopi might do it because that windmill is *kahopi.*" It was one of perhaps a dozen Hopi words Chee had picked up so far. It meant something like "anti-Hopi," or the reverse-positive of Hopi values.

Cowboy translated. This time Sawkatewa responded at some length, his eyes shifting from Cowboy to Chee and back again.

"What are you leading up to with all this?" Cowboy asked. "You think this old man sabotaged the windmill?"

"What'd he say?" Chee asked.

"He said that the Hopis are a prayerful people. He said many of them have gone the wrong way, and follow the ways the white men teach, and try to let the Tribal Council run things instead of the way we were taught when we emerged from the underworld. But he said that the prayers are working again tonight. He said the cloud will bring water blessings to the Hopis tonight."

"Tell him I said that we Navajos share in this blessing, and are thankful."

Cowboy repeated it. The boy came in and put a white coffee mug on the floor beside the old man. He handed Cowboy a Styrofoam cup and Chee a Ronald McDonald soft-drink glass. The light of the kerosene lamp gave his waxy white skin a yellow cast and reflected off the thick lenses of his wire-rimmed glasses. He disappeared through the doorway without speaking.

The old man was speaking again.

Cowboy looked into his cup, cleared his throat. "He said that even if he had been there, he was told that the plane crashed at night. He asks how could anyone see anything?"

"Maybe he couldn't," Chee said.

"But you think he was there?"

"I know he was there," Chee said. "I'd bet my life on it."

Cowboy looked at Chee, waiting. The boy returned with a steaming aluminum pan. He poured coffee from it into the old man's mug, and Cowboy's Styrofoam cup, and Chee's McDonald's glass.

"Tell him," Chee said, looking directly at Sawkatewa, "that my uncle taught me that certain things are forbidden. He taught me that the Navajos and the Hopis agree on certain things and that one of those is that we must respect our mother earth. Like the Hopis, we have places which bring us blessings and are sacred. Places where we collect the things we need for our medicine bundles."

Chee turned to Cowboy. "Tell him that. Then I will go on."

Cowboy translated. The old man sipped his coffee, listening. Chee sipped his. It was instant coffee, boiled in water which tasted a little of gypsum and a little of rust from the barrel in which it was stored. Cowboy finished. Again there was a rumble of thunder and suddenly the pounding of hail on the roof over their heads. The old man smiled. The albino, leaning in the doorway now, smiled too. The hail converted itself quickly into rain—heavy, hard-falling drops, but not quite as noisy. Chee raised his voice slightly. "There is a place near the windmill where the earth has blessed the Hopis with water. And the Hopis have repaid the blessing

143

by giving the spirit of the earth there *pahos*. That has been done for a long, long time. But then people did a *kahopi* thing. They drilled a well in the earth and drained away the water from the sacred place. And the spirit of the spring stopped providing water. And then he refused the offering of the *paho*. When it was offered, the spirit knocked it down. Now, we Navajos, too, are peaceful people. Not as peaceful as the Hopis, perhaps, but peaceful. But even so, my uncle taught me that we must protect our sacred places. If this had been a shrine of the Navajos, if this had been a shrine left for me to protect, then I would protect it." Chee nodded. Cowboy translated. Sawkatewa sipped his coffee again.

"There are higher laws than the white man's law," Chee said.

Sawkatewa nodded, without waiting for Cowboy to translate. He spoke to the boy, who disappeared into the darkness and returned in a moment with three cigarets. He handed one to each of them, took the chimney off the lamp and passed it around to give each of them a light from the wick. Sawkatewa inhaled hugely and let a plume of smoke emerge from the corner of his mouth. Chee puffed lightly. He didn't want a cigaret. The dampness of the rain had flooded into the room, filling it with the smell of water, the ozone of the lightning, the aroma of dampened dust, sage, and the thousand other desert things which release perfume when raindrops strike them. But this smoke had ceremonial meaning somehow. Chee would not alienate the old man. He would smoke skunk cabbage rather than break this mood.

Finally Sawkatewa stood up. He put the cigaret aside. He held his hands before him, palms down, about waist level, and he began speaking. He spoke for almost five minutes.

"I won't translate all of it now," Cowboy said. "He went all the way back to the time when the Hopi emerged into this world through the *sipapuni* and found that Masaw had been appointed guardian of this world. And he tells how

Masaw let each of the kinds of peoples pick their way of life, and how the Navajo picked the long ear of soft corn for the easy life and the Hopi picked the short, hard ear so that they would always have hard times but would always endure. And then he tells about how Masaw formed each of the clans, and how the Water Clan was formed, and how the Fog Clan split off from the Water, and all that. I'm not going to translate all that. His point is—"

"If you don't translate for about three or four minutes, he's going to know you're cheating," Chee said. "Go ahead and translate. What's the rush?"

So Cowboy translated. Chee heard of the migrations to the end of the continent in the west, and the end of the continent to the east, and the frozen door of the earth to the north, and the other end of the earth to the south. He told how the Fog Clan had left its footprints in the form of abandoned stone villages and cliff dwellings in all directions, and how it had come to make its alliance with the animal people, and how the animal people had joined the clan, and taught them the ceremony to perform so that people could keep their animal hearts as well as their human hearts and change back and forth by passing through the magic hoop. He told how the Fog Clan had finally completed its great cycle of migrations and come to Oraibi and asked the Bear Clan for a village site, and land to grow its corn, and hunting grounds where it could collect the eagles it needed for its ceremonials. He told how the *kikmongwi* at Oraibi had at first refused, but had agreed when the clan had offered to add its Ya Ya ceremonial to the religion of the Hopis. Cowboy stopped finally, and sipped the last of his coffee.

"I'm getting hoarse," he said. "And that's about it anyway. At the end he said, yes, there are higher laws than the white man's. He said the law of the white man is of no concern to a Hopi. He said for a Hopi, or a Navajo, to involve himself in the affairs of white men is not good. He said that even if he did not believe this, it was dark when the plane crashed. He said he cannot see in the dark."

"Did he say exactly that. That he can't see in the dark?"

Cowboy looked surprised. "Well," he said. "Let's see. He said why do you think he could see in the dark?"

Chee thought about it. The gusting wind drove the rain against the windowpane and whined around the roof corners.

"Tell him that what he says is good. It is not good for a Navajo or a Hopi to involve himself in white affairs. But tell him that this time there is no choice for us. Navajos and Hopis have been involved. You and I. And tell him that if he will tell us what he saw, we will tell him something that will be useful for keeping the shrine."

"We will?" Cowboy said. "What?"

"Go ahead and translate," Chee said. "And also say this. Say I think he can see in the dark because my uncle taught me that it is one of the gifts you receive when you step through the hoop of the Ya Ya. Like the animals, your eyes know no darkness."

Cowboy looked doubtful. "I'm not sure I want to tell him that."

"Tell him," Chee said.

Cowboy translated. Chee noticed the albino listening at the doorway. The albino looked nervous. But Sawkatewa smiled.

He spoke.

"He says what can you tell him? He's calling your bluff."

He'd won! Chee felt exultance. There'd been no bargaining now. The agreement had been reached.

"Tell him I said that I know it is very hard to break the windmill. The first time was easy. The bolts come loose and the windmill is pulled over and it takes a long time to undo the damage. The second time it was easy again. An iron bar stuck into the gearbox. The third time it was not so

146

bad. The pump rod is bent and it destroys itself. But now the bolts cannot be removed, and the gearbox is protected, and soon the pump rod will be protected, too. Next time it will be very hard to damage the windmill. Ask him if that is not true."

Cowboy translated. Taylor Sawkatewa simply stared at Chee, waiting.

"If I were the guardian of the shrine," Chee said, "or if I owed a favor to the guardian of the shrine, as I will when he tells me what he saw when the plane crashed, I would buy a sack of cement. I would haul the sack of cement to the windmill and I would leave it there along with a sack full of sand and a tub full of water and a little plastic funnel. If I was the man who owed the favor, I would leave all that there and drive away. And if I was the guardian of the shrine, I would mix up the cement and sand and water into a paste a little thinner than the dough one makes for *piki* bread and I would pour a little through the funnel down into the windmill shaft, and I would then wait a few minutes for it to dry, and then I would pour a little more, and I would do that until all the cement was in the well, and the well was sealed up solid as a rock."

Cowboy's face was incredulous. "I'm not going to tell him that," he said.

"Why not?" Chee asked.

Sawkatewa said something in Hopi. Cowboy responded tersely.

"He got some of it," Cowboy said. "Why not? Because, God damn it, just think about it a minute."

"Who's going to know but us?" Chee asked. "You like that windmill?"

Cowboy shrugged.

"Then tell him."

Cowboy translated. Sawkatewa listened intently, his eyes on Chee.

Then he spoke three words.

"He wants to know when."

"Tell him I want to buy the cement away from the reservation—maybe in Cameron or Flagstaff. Tell him it will be at the windmill two nights from now."

Cowboy told him. The old man's hands rediscovered the wool and the spindle in the beer carton and resumed their work. Cowboy and Chee waited. The old man didn't speak until he had filled the spindle. Then he spoke for a long time.

"He said it is true he can see pretty good in the dark, but not as good as when he was a boy. He said he heard someone driving up Wepo Wash and he went down there to see what was happening. When he got there a man was putting out a row of lanterns on the sand, with another man holding a gun on him. When this was finished, the man who had put out the lanterns sat beside the car and the other man stood there, still pointing the gun." Cowboy stopped abruptly, asked a question, and got an answer.

"It was a little gun, he says. A pistol. In a little while an airplane came over very low to the ground and the man on the ground got up and flashed a flashlight off and on. Little later, the plane came back again. Fellow flashes his light again, and then—just after the airplane crashes—the man with the pistol shoots the man with the flashlight. The airplane hit the rock. The man with the gun takes the flashlight and looks around the airplane some. Then he goes and collects all the lanterns and puts them in the car, except for one. That one he leaves on the rock so he can see something. Then he starts taking things out of the airplane. Then he puts the body of the man he shot up against the rock and gets into the car and drives away. Then Sawkatewa says he went to the plane to see, and he hears you running up, so he goes away."

"What did the man unload out of the airplane?"

Cowboy relayed the question. Sawkatewa made a shape

148

with his hands, perhaps thirty inches long, perhaps eighteen inches high, and provided a description in Hopi with a few English words thrown in. Chee recognized "aluminum" and "suitcase."

"He said there were two things that looked like aluminum suitcases. About so"—Cowboy demonstrated an aluminum suitcase with his hands—"by so."

"He didn't say what he did with them," Chee said. "Put them in the car, I guess."

Cowboy asked.

Sawkatewa shook his head. Spoke. Cowboy looked surprised.

"He said he didn't think he put them in the car."

"Didn't put the suitcases in the car? What the hell did he do with them?"

Sawkatewa spoke again without awaiting a translation.

"He said he disappeared in the dark with them. Just gone a little while. Off in the darkness where he couldn't see anything."

"How long is a little while? Three minutes? Five? It couldn't have been very long. I got there about twenty minutes after the plane hit."

Cowboy relayed the question. Sawkatewa shrugged. Thought. Said something.

"About as long as it takes to boil an egg hard. That's what he says."

"What did the man look like?"

Sawkatewa had not been close enough to see him well in the bad light. He saw only shape and movement.

Outside, the rain had gone now. Drifted off to the east. They could hear it muttering its threats and promises back over Black Mesa. But the village stones dripped with water, and muddy rivulets ran here and there over the stone track, and the rocks reflected wet in the headlights of Cowboy's

149

car. Maybe a quarter inch, Chee thought. A heavy shower, but not a real rain. Enough to dampen the dust, and wash things off, and help a little. Most important, there had to be a first rain before the rainy season could get going.

"You think he knows what he's talking about?" Cowboy asked. "You think that guy didn't load the dope into the car?"

"I think he told us what he saw," Chee said.

"Doesn't make sense," Cowboy said. He pulled the patrol car out of a skid on the slick track. "You really going to haul that cement out there for him to plug up the well?"

"I refuse to answer on grounds that it might tend to incriminate me," Chee said.

"Hell," Cowboy said. "That won't do me any good. You got me in so deep now, I'm just going to pretend I never heard any of that."

"I'll pretend, too," Chee said.

"If he didn't haul those suitcases off in that car, how the devil did he haul them out?"

"I don't know," Chee said. "Maybe he didn't."

22

Chee had noticed the tracks when he first turned off the asphalt onto the graded dirt road which passed the Burnt Water Trading post and wandered northeastward up Wepo Wash. The tracks meant only that someone was up even earlier than he was. They meant a vehicle had come this way since last night's shower. It was only when he noticed the tread marks on the damp sand on the wash bottom that he became interested. He stopped his pickup and got out for a closer look. The tires were almost new, the tread common to heavy passenger cars and pickup trucks. Chee memorized them, more from habit than intention, the reflex of a life way in which memory is important. Deputy Sheriff Dashee might be making this trip this morning, but Dashee's tires were Goodyears and this tread Firestone. Who would be driving up Wepo Wash at dawn? Where would they be going, except to the site of the plane crash? Ironfingers returning to the scene of his crime? Chee drove slowly, keeping his engine noise down and his eyes open. As soon as the early light permitted, he flicked off his headlights. Twice he stopped and listened. He heard nothing except the sound of morning birds, busy with their first post-rain day. He stopped again, at the place where a side arroyo provided the exit route to the track that led to his windmill. The fresh tire tracks continued upwash. Chee pulled his pickup to the right, up the arroyo. He had a good official reason to visit the windmill. He'd been warned to stay away from the airplane.

A flock of crows had occupied the windmill area and the sentinel, perched atop the stationary directional vane, cawed out a raucous alarm as Chee drove up. He parked, more or less out of sight, behind the water tank, and walked directly to the shrine. The parched earth had soaked in most of the rain, but the fall had been abrupt enough to produce runoff an inch or so deep down the arroyo bottom, sweeping it clean. There were no fresh tracks.

Chee took his time, making frequent stops to listen. He was near the point where the arroyo drained into Wepo Wash when he first saw footprints. He inspected them. Someone had walked about one hundred fifty yards up the arroyo, and then down again. The arroyo mouth was a bit less than a quarter mile upwash from the crash site. Chee stood behind the heavy brush which had flourished there. A white Chevy Blazer was parked by the wreckage. Two men were in view. He recognized Collins, the blond who'd handcuffed him in his trailer, but the other man was only vaguely familiar. He was heavyset, a little short of middle age and beginning to show it, dressed in khaki pants and shirt and wearing a long-billed cap. He and Collins were about fifty yards apart. They were searching along the opposite bank of the wash, poking into the brush and examining crevices. Collins was working downwash, away from where Chee stood. The other man moved upwash toward Chee. Where had he seen him before? It seemed to have been recently, or fairly so. Probably another federal cop from somewhere. While he thought about it, he heard footsteps on the sand.

Chee ducked back into the brush, squatting to make himself less visible. From that position, he could see only part of the man who walked just past the mouth of the arroyo. But he saw enough to recognize Johnson, walking slowly, carrying a driftwood stick.

Johnson stopped. Chee couldn't see his upper torso, but the way his hips pivoted, the man seemed to be looking up the arroyo. Chee tensed. Held his breath. Then Johnson turned away.

"Finding anything?"

Chee heard only one answer. A voice, which might have been Collins's, shouting, "Nothing."

Johnson's legs moved quickly out of view down the wash.

Chee moved back to the mouth of the arroyo, cautious. Until he could locate Johnson, the man might be anywhere. He heard the DEA agent's voice near the crash site and breathed easier. He could see all three men now, standing under the uptilted wing, apparently discussing things. Then they climbed into the vehicle, Johnson driving. With a spinning of wheels on the damp sand, it made a sweeping turn and roared off down the wash. If they'd found any aluminum suitcases, they hadn't loaded them into the Blazer.

Chee spent a quarter of an hour making sure he knew where and how Johnson and friends had searched. Last night's runoff down Wepo Wash had been shallow but it had swept the sand clean. Every mark made this morning was as easy to see as a chalk mark on a clean blackboard. Johnson and friends had made a careful search up and down the cliffs of the wash and around the basalt upthrust. Brush had been poked under, driftwood moved, crevices examined. No place in which a medium-sized suitcase might have been hidden was overlooked.

Chee sat under the wing and thought his thoughts. In the wake of the shower the morning was humid, with patches of fog still being burned off the upper slopes of Big Mountain. A few wispy white clouds already were signaling that it might be another afternoon of thunderheads. He took his notebook out of his pocket and reread the notes he'd made yesterday. On the section where he'd written "Dashee" he

153

added another remark: "Johnson learns immediately what old Hopi told us. How?"

He looked at the question. When Cowboy had returned to Flagstaff he'd typed up a report, just as Chee had done at Tuba City. Johnson obviously had learned about the suitcases during the night. From Dashee? From whoever was on night duty at the sheriff's office?

Chee closed the notebook and muttered a Navajo imprecation. What difference did it make? He wasn't really suspicious of Cowboy. His thinking was going in all the wrong directions. "Everything has a right direction to it," his uncle would have told him. "You need to do it *sunwise*. From the east, toward the south, to the west, and finally around to the north. That's the way the sun goes, that's the way you turn when you walk into a hogan, that's the way everything works. That's the way you should think." And what the devil did his uncle's abstract Navajo generality mean in this case? It meant, Chee thought, that you should start in the beginning, and work your way around to the end.

So where was the beginning? People with cocaine in Mexico. People in the United States who wanted to buy it. And someone who worked for one group or the other, who knew of a good, secret place to land an airplane. Joseph Musket or young West, or maybe even both of them plus the elder West. Musket is released from prison, and comes to Burnt Water, and sets up the landing.

Chee paused, sorting it out.

Then the DEA gets wind of something. Johnson visits West at the prison, threatens him, sets him up to be killed.

Chee paused again, fished out the notebook, turned to the proper place, and scribbled in: "Johnson sets up West to be killed? If so, why?"

Then, a couple of days later, John Doe is killed on Black Mesa, maybe by Ironfingers Musket. Maybe by a witch. Or maybe Ironfingers is a witch. Or maybe there was absolutely no connection between Doe and anything else. Maybe he was simply a stray, an accidental victim of evil. Maybe. Chee doubted it. Nothing in his Navajo conditioning prepared him to accept happily the fact that coincidences sometimes happen.

He skipped past Doe, leaving everything about him unresolved, and came to the night of the crash. Three men must have been in the GMC when it arrived. One of them must have been already dead. A corpse already seated in the back seat and the other man a prisoner held at pistol point. Held by Ironfingers? Two outsiders coming in to oversee the delivery of the cocaine. Meeting Musket to be guided to the landing site. Musket killing one, keeping the other one alive. Why? Because only this man knew how to signal a safe landing to the pilot. That would be why. And after the signal had been flashed, killing the man. Why would Ironfingers leave one body and hide the other? To give the owners of the dope a misleading impression about who had stolen it? Possibly. Chee thought about it. The business about the body had bothered Chee from the first and it bothered him now. Musket, or whoever had been the driver, must have planned to bury it eventually. Why else the shovel? But why bury it when it would be easier to carry it back into some arroyo and leave it for the scavengers?

Chee got up, took out his pocket knife, and opened its longest blade. With that, he probed into the bed of the wash near where he had sat. The blade sank easily into the damp sand. But two inches below the surface, the earth was compact. He looked around him. The basalt upthrust was a barrier around which runoff water swirled. There the bottom would be irregular. In some places the current would cut deeply after hard rains, only to have the holes filled in by the slower drainage after lesser storms. Chee climbed out of the wash and hurried back to his pickup at the windmill. From behind the front seat he extracted the jack handle—

a long steel bar bent at one end to provide leverage for a lug wrench socket and flattened into a narrow blade at the other to facilitate prying off hub caps. Chee took it back to the wash.

It took just a few minutes to find what he was looking for. The place had to be behind the basalt, because old Taylor Sawkatewa had said the man who unloaded the suitcases had taken them out of sight in the darkness. Chee probed into the damp sand no more than twenty times before he struck aluminum.

There was the thunk of steel on the thin metal of the case. Chee probed again, and again, and found the second case. He knelt and dug back the sand with his hand. The cases were buried upright, side by side, with their handles no more than six inches below the surface.

Chee carefully refilled the little holes his jack handle had made, replaced the sand he had dug away with his hands, patted it to the proper firmness, and then took out his handkerchief and brushed away the traces he'd left on the surface. Then he walked over the cache. It felt no different from the undisturbed sand. Finally he spent almost an hour making himself a little broom of rabbit brush and carefully erasing the tracks of Jimmy Chee from the bottom of Wepo Wash. If anyone ever tracked him, they'd find only that he had come down the arroyo to the wash, and the gone back up it again to the windmill. And driven away.

23

The dispatcher reached Chee just as he turned off the Burnt Water–Wepo Wash road onto the pavement of Navajo Route 3. She had a tip from the Arizona Highway Patrol. One of their units had watched Priscilla Bisti and her boys loading six cases of wine into her pickup truck at Winslow that morning. Mrs. Bisti had been observed driving northward toward the Navajo Reservation on Arizona 58.

"What time?"

"About ten-fourteen," the dispatcher said.

"Anything else?"

"No."

"Can you check my desk and see if I got any telephone messages?"

"I'm not supposed to," the dispatcher said. The dispatcher was Shirley Topaha. Shirley Topaha was just two years out of Tuba City High School, where she had been a cheerleader for the Tuba City Tigers. She had pretty eyes, and very white teeth, and perfect skin, and a plump figure. Chee had noticed all this, along with her tendency to flirt with all officers, visitors, prisoners, etc., requiring only that they be male.

"The captain won't notice it," Chee said. "It might save me a lot of time. It would really be nice if you did."

"I'll call you back," the dispatcher said.

That came about five minutes later. It came about two

minutes after Chee had turned his patrol car westward toward Moenkopi and Tuba City. Which was too bad, because it meant he had to stop and turn around.

"Two calls," Shirley said. "One says call Johnson, Drug Enforcement Agency, and there's this number in Flagstaff." She gave him the number. "And the other says please call Miss Pauling at the Hopi motel."

"Thanks, Shirley," Chee said.

"Ten-four," said Shirley.

The man at the desk of the Hopi Cultural Center motel rang Miss Pauling's telephone five times and declared that she wasn't in. Chee checked the motel dining room. She was sitting at a corner table, a cup of coffee in front of her, immersed in a Phoenix *Gazette.*

"You left a call for me," Chee said. "Did Gaines come back?"

"Yes," Miss Pauling said. "Sit down. Do you know how to tap a telephone?" She looked intense, excited.

"Tap a telephone?" Chee sat down. "What's going on?"

"There was a message for Gaines," Miss Pauling said. "Someone called and left it. They'd call back at four, and if he wanted me to make an arrangement, to be in his room to take the call."

"The clerk showed you the message?"

"Sure," she said. "He checked us in together, and we got adjoining rooms. But we don't have much time." She glanced at her watch. "Less than half an hour. Can we get the telephone tapped?"

"Miss Pauling," Chee said. "This is Second Mesa, Arizona. I don't know how to tap a telephone."

"I think it's easy," she said.

"It looks easy on television," Chee said. "But you have to have some sort of equipment. And you have to know how."

"You could call somebody?"

158

"Not and get a telephone tapped in anything less than about three days," Chee said. "In the Navajo Police, it's out of our line of work. If you call the FBI in Phoenix, they'd know how, but they'd have to get a court order." And then, Chee thought, there's Johnson of the DEA, who wouldn't worry about a court order, and would probably have the equipment in his hip pocket. He wondered why Johnson wanted him to call. Whatever, it was a call he didn't intend to make.

Miss Pauling looked stricken. She worried her lower lip with her teeth.

"How about just listening at the wall?" Chee asked. "Where do they put the telephones? Could you hear from one room to the next?"

Miss Pauling thought about it. "I doubt it," she said. "Not even if he talked loud."

Chee glanced at his watch. It was 3:33 P.M. In twenty-seven minutes, more or less, Ironfingers would be calling Ben Gaines, making arrangements to trade two aluminum suitcases full of cocaine for . . . for what? Probably for a huge amount of money. Whatever he exchanged it for, Musket would have to name a time and a place. Chee wished fervently that he had the clips and the earphones, or whatever it took to eavesdrop on a telephone call.

"Could we tell the guy at the switchboard that when the call came, Gaines would be in your room? Have him put it through your telephone?"

"Wouldn't work," Miss Pauling said.

Chee had seen it wouldn't work as soon as he'd said it. "Not unless I could imitate Gaines's voice."

Miss Pauling shook her head. "You couldn't," she said.

"I guess not," Chee said. He thought.

"What are you thinking about? Anything helpful?"

"No," Chee said. "I was thinking it would be good if we could get in the back of that telephone switchboard and

159

somehow do some splicing with the wires." He shrugged, dismissing the thought.

"No," Miss Pauling said. "I think it's a GTE board. It takes tools."

Chee looked at her, surprised. "GTE board?"

"I think so. It looked like the one we had at the high school."

"You know something about switchboards?"

"I used to operate one. For about a year. Along with filing, a lot of other things."

"You could operate this one?"

"Anybody can operate a switchboard," she said. "If you're smart enough to dress yourself." She laughed. "It's certainly not skilled labor. Three minutes of instructions and . . ." She let it trail off.

"And the switchboard operator can listen in on the calls?"

"Sure," she said, frowning at him. "But they're not going to let . . ."

"How much time do we have?" Chee said. "I'll cause some sort of distraction to get that Hopi away from there, and you handle the call."

Later, several possibilities occurred to Chee that were much better than starting a fire. Less flamboyant, less risky, and the same effect. But at the moment he only had about twenty minutes. The only creative thought he had was fire.

He handed Miss Pauling a ten-dollar bill. "Pay the check," he said. "Be near the switchboard. Two or three minutes before four, I come running in and get the clerk out of there."

The raw material he needed was just where he remembered seeing it. A great pile of tumbleweeds had drifted into a corner behind the cultural center museum. Chee inspected the pile apprehensively. It was still a little damp from the previous night's shower but—being tumbleweed— it would burn with a furious red heat, damp or not. And the pile was slightly bigger than he remembered. Chee glanced around nervously. The weeds were piled into the junction of two of the cement-block walls which formed the back of the museum, conveniently out of sight. He hoped no one had seen him. He imagined the headline. NAVAJO COP NAILED FOR HOPI ARSON. OFFICER CHARGED WITH TORCHING CULTURAL CENTER. He imagined trying to explain this to Captain Largo. But there wasn't time to think of it. A quick look around, and he struck a match. He held it low under the prickly gray mass of weed stems. The tumbleweed, which always burned at a flash, merely caught, winked out, smoldered, caught again, smoldered, caught again, smoldered. Chee lit another match, tried a drier spot, looked nervously at his watch. Less than six minutes. The tumbleweed caught; flame flared through it, producing a sudden heat and smoggy white smoke. Chee stepped back and fanned it furiously with his uniform hat. (If anyone is watching this, he thought, I'll never get out of jail.) The fire was crackling now, producing the chain reaction of heat. Hat in hand, Chee sprinted for the motel office.

He ran through the door, up to the desk. The clerk, a young man, was talking to an older Hopi woman.

"Hate to interrupt," he said, "but something's burning out there!"

The Hopis looked at him politely.

"Burning?" the clerk said.

"Burning," Chee said loudly. "There's smoke coming over the roof. I think the building's burning."

"Burning!" the Hopi shouted. He came around the desk at a run. Miss Pauling was standing at the coffee shop entrance, watching tensely.

The fire was eating furiously into the tumbleweeds when they rounded the corner. The clerk took it in at a glance.

"Try to pull it away from the wall," he shouted at Chee. "I'll get water."

Chee looked at his watch. Three minutes to four. Had he started it too early? He stomped at the weeds with his boots, kicking a section of the unburned pile aside to retard the spread. And then the Hopi was back, bringing two buckets of water and two other men. The tumbleweeds now were burning with the furious resinous heat common of desert plants. Chee fought fire with a will now, inhaling a lungful of acrid smoke, coughing, eyes watering. In what seemed like just a minute, it was over. The clerk was throwing a last bucketful of water over the last smoking holdout. One of the helpers was examining places where embers had produced burn holes in his jeans. Chee rubbed watering eyes.

"I wonder what could have started it," Chee said. "You wouldn't think that stuff would burn like that after that rain."

"Goddamn tumbleweeds," the Hopi said. "I wonder what did start it." He was looking at Chee. Chee thought he detected a trace of suspicion.

"Maybe a cigaret," he said. He started poking through the blackened remains with his foot. The fire had lasted a little longer than it seemed. It was four minutes after four.

"Blackened up the wall," the Hopi said, inspecting it. "Have to be repainted." He turned to walk back to the motel office.

"Somebody ought to check the roof," Chee said. "The flames were going up over the parapet."

The Hopi stopped and looked toward the flat roof. His expression was skeptical.

"No smoke," he said. "It's all right. That roof would still be damp."

"I thought I saw smoke," Chee said. "Be hell if that tarred roof caught on fire. Is there a way to get up there?"

"I guess I better check," the clerk said. He headed off in the other direction at a fast walk. To get a ladder, Chee guessed. He hoped the ladder was a long ways off.

Miss Pauling was coming, hurried and nervous, from be-

162

hind the counter when Chee pushed through the door. Her face was white. She looked flustered.

Chee rushed her outside to his patrol car. The clerk was hurrying across the patio, carrying an aluminum ladder.

"Call come?"

She nodded, still speechless.

"Anybody see you?"

"Just a couple of customers," she said. "They wanted to pay their lunch tickets. I told them to just leave the money on the counter. Was that all right?"

"All right with me," Chee said. He held the car door for her, let himself in on the driver's side. Neither of them said anything until he pulled out of the parking lot and was on the highway.

Then Miss Pauling laughed. "Isn't that funny," she said. "I haven't been so terrified since I was a girl."

"It is funny," Chee said. "I'm still nervous."

Miss Pauling laughed again. "I think you're terrified of how embarrassed you're going to be. What are you going to say if that man comes back and there you are behind his counter playing switchboard operator?"

"Exactly," Chee said. "What are you going to say if he says, 'Hey, there, what are you doing burning down my cultural center?'"

Miss Pauling got her nerves under control. "But the call did come through," she said.

"It must have been short," Chee said.

"Thank God," she said fervently.

"What'd you learn?"

"It was a man," Miss Pauling said. "He asked for Gaines, and Gaines answered the phone on the first ring, and the man asked him if he wanted the suitcases back, and—"

"He said suitcases?"

"Suitcases," Miss Pauling confirmed. "And Gaines said yes, they did, and the man said that could be arranged. And then he said it would cost five hundred thousand dollars, and they would have to be in tens and twenties and not in consecutive order, in two briefcases, and he said they would have to be delivered by The Boss himself. And Gaines said that would be a problem, and the man said either The Boss or no deal, and Gaines said it would take some time. He said it would take at least twenty-four hours. And the man said they would have more than that. He said the trade would be made at nine P.M. two nights after tonight."

"Friday night," Chee said.

"Friday night," Miss Pauling agreed. "Then the man said to be ready for nine P.M. Friday night, and he hung up."

"That's all of it?"

"Oh, the man said he'd be back in touch to tell Gaines where they'd meet. And *then* he hung up."

"But he didn't name the place?"

"He didn't."

"Say anything else?"

"That's the substance of it."

"He explain why the boss had to deliver the money?"

"He said he didn't trust anybody else. He said if the boss was there himself, nobody would risk trying anything funny."

"Any names mentioned?"

"Oh, yes," Miss Pauling said. "The man called Gaines Gaines and once Gaines said something like 'Palanzer.' He said something like: 'I don't see why you're doing this, Palanzer. You would have made almost that much.' That was after the man—Palanzer, I guess—said he wanted the five hundred thousand."

"What did the man say to that?"

"He just laughed. Or it sounded like a laugh. His voice sounded muffled all through the conversation—like he was talking with something in his mouth."

"Or with something over his mouth." Chee paused. "He specified nine P.M.?"

Miss Pauling nodded. "He said, 'Exactly nine P.M.'"

Chee pulled off the asphalt, made a backing turn, and headed back toward the motel. He smelled of smoke.

"Well," Miss Pauling said. "Now we know who has it, and when they're going to make the switch."

"But not where," Chee said. Why the muffled voice, he was asking himself. Because the caller would have been good old Ironfingers, and because Ironfingers would want Gaines to believe the caller was Palanzer. Joseph Musket, despite his years of living among whites, would not have lost his breathy Navajo pronunciation.

"How do we find out where?"

"That's going to take some thinking," Chee said.

24

◆

Thinking didn't seem to help. Chee went to sleep that night thinking. He got up the next morning and went over to his office, still deep in thought. His only conclusion was that he must be thinking the wrong way. There was nothing much in his In basket except a note that Johnson of the DEA was trying to reach him and a carbon of the report on the Burnt Water necklace turning up. It simply repeated what Dashee had told him, with the details filled in.

Subject named Edna Nezzie, twenty-three, unmarried, of the Graywoman Nezzie camp, north of Teec Nos Pos, had pawned the necklace at Mexican Water. It had been recognized from the description left with the post manager by Tribal Police. Subsequently, subject Nezzie had told investigating officer Eddie Begay that she had been given the necklace by a male subject she had met two nights earlier at a squaw dance next to Mexican Water. She identified the subject as a Navajo male about thirty, who had identified himself as Joseph Musket. The two had gone to a white Ford pickup Musket was driving. There they had engaged in sexual intercourse. Musket then had given the subject the necklace and they had returned to the dance. She had seen no more of him.

Chee frowned at the paper, trying to identify why something was wrong about it. Still staring at the report, he fumbled for the telephone, and dailed the operator, and asked for the number of the trading post at Teec Nos Pos. It rang five times before he got an answer.

Chee identified himself. "Just need some information. What clan is Graywoman Nezzie?"

"Nezzie," the voice said. "She's born to Standing Rock and born for Bitter Water."

"You're sure?"

"I'm one of the old lady's sons-in-law," the voice said. "Married into 'em. The father is Water Runs Together and Many Poles."

"Thanks," Chee said, and hung up. He remembered Mrs. Musket identifying herself. Born to Standing Rock Dinee, she had said, and born for the Mud Clan. So the man who had identified himself as Joseph Musket at the Mexican Water squaw dance could not possibly have been Joseph Musket. For a Navajo male to dance with a Navajo female of the same maternal clan violated the most stringent of taboos. And the intra-clan intercourse that followed was the most heinous form of incest—sure to cause sickness, sure to cause insanity, likely to bring death. If it was Musket, it could only mean that he had lied to the girl about his clan. Otherwise she would never have danced with him, gone to the truck with him, even talked to him except in the most formal fashion. And no Navajo male would engage in such a ghastly deception.

Unless, Chee thought, he was a witch.

Chee left a note to tell Largo where to find him and headed for Cameron. En route he remembered what Mrs. Musket had told him about the homecoming of Ironfingers, his urgent need for the traditional Navajo purification ceremonial, his stated intentions to rejoin the People as a herder of sheep. Such behavior was incongruous with deliberate incest—an act which any traditional Navajo knew endangered the health of the entire clan. Chee narrowed it down to two choices. Either someone had imitated Ironfingers at the

167

squaw dance, or Ironfingers was a madman. Or in other words, a witch.

In Cameron he bought a sack of cement at the lumberyard, and a tub at the hardware store, and a flexible plastic funnel at the drugstore. Then he made the long, lonely drive back to the Hopi Reservation, still thinking. At the windmill he left the sack of cement beside the well shaft, put the funnel beside it, and covered both with the tub, just in case the rain clouds building up again in the west produced some moisture.

He drove back down Wepo Wash to Burnt Water Trading Post and parked in the shade of the cottonwood beside West's battered and rusty jeep. By then he had come up with only a single idea. He could stake out the cache of suitcases and nail Musket when he came to dig them up. It wasn't a very good idea. Chee didn't think he could count on Musket coming for the suitcases. More likely, Ironfingers would collect his money and tell the buyers where to pick up the goods. Chee was not interested in the buyers. He was officially, formally, and by explicit orders not interested. But Ironfingers was his business. He had been told to solve the burglary at Burnt Water. He had been told to unravel the business of witchcraft on Black Mesa. Ironfingers was the answer to the first. Ironfingers might have some answers to the second.

Chee sat. He watched the thunderheads boiling up in the west. He went through it all again. The conclusion was the same. Musket would have to come to whatever meeting place he established to get his money. He would not be likely to go dig up the suitcases. The crash scene must seem dangerous to him. Musket couldn't tell Gaines where to meet him until the last moment—to do so could give the buyers a chance to set up a trap. Chee could think of no possible way he could intercept the information. He had thought of digging up the suitcases himself, rehiding them somewhere, and leaving a note to force Musket to come to him. But more likely it would be the buyers who would find the note and come to him. That was the sort of trouble Chee didn't intend to invite. In fact, it was the sort of trouble that had been at the back of his mind ever since Johnson had warned him that the drug dealers would be looking for him. Johnson's prediction hadn't proved true—but still might. The people for whom Gaines worked might well guess that Palanzer would have needed a local helper. There was no way for Chee to know for sure that they knew about Ironfingers.

Chee fished out his notebook and reexamined what he had written while waiting for Cowboy Dashee. "Where is J. Musket?" He stared at the question. And then at another. "Why the burglary?" And then at "Who is John Doe?" He thought about the dates. Doe had died July 10, young West had died July 6. Musket had walked out of this trading post two weeks later and vanished—apparently after coming back the same night to haul off a load of pawn jewelry. Then, weeks later, he carelessly gives away a single piece. Or someone gives it away in Musket's name.

Chee climbed out of his truck and walked into the trading post. If West wasn't occupied, he'd go over the whole burglary business with him again.

West was putting an order of groceries and odds and ends into a box for a middle-aged Navajo woman. The purchase included a coil of that light, flexible rope which Navajos used to tie sheep, horses, loads on pickup trucks, and all those thousands of things which must be tied. West had left the coil for last. Now he dropped it into the box, said something to the woman, and took it out again. He measured out fifteen or twenty feet of it with quick outthrusts of his arms, and then collected this in a tangle of loops in his right hand, talking to the woman all the time. Still standing at the doorway, Chee couldn't overhear what he was saying.

Whatever it was, it attracted two men who had been standing down the counter. West handed the woman the rope. All three Navajos inspected it. They were grinning. West the sorcerer was about to perform. He took the rope back, folded it into a half-dozen dangling loops in his huge right hand. His left hand extracted a knife from his coveralls pocket. He slashed through the loops, and held up eight cut ends. Then he disposed of the knife, extracted a bandanna from his pocket, covered the severed ends with the handkerchief. He was talking steadily. Chee guessed he was explaining the curing quality of his magic handkerchief. A moment later West pulled the bandanna away and with the same motion dropped the rope. It fell to the floor, a single piece again. West whipped it up, snapped it between his outstretched hands. He handed it to the woman. She inspected it, and was impressed. The two male watchers were grinning appreciatively. Chee grinned, too. A good trick, well done. He'd seen it before—a magic show done for donations on the Union Mall at the University of New Mexico. It had taken him most of the day to narrow down the only possible way the trick could be done. And that night he'd gone to the library, and found a book of magic tricks in the stacks, and confirmed that he'd been right. The trick was in creating the illusion with the gathered loops that the cord had been cut into fragments when actually only short bits had been sliced from one end—and those disposed of in a pocket when the bandanna was whipped away.

Chee stood by the doorway, remembering the three of diamonds trick, which also depended on creating an illusion—the distracting thought that it mattered which card the victim named. West was a master of this business of controlling how one thought. A master of illusion.

Chee's smile faded. His face fell into that slack, mindless appearance of totally concentrated thought. Slowly the smile appeared again, and broadened, and converted itself into a great, exultant laugh. It was loud enough to attract West's attention. He was looking at Chee, surprised. His audience was also staring.

"You want to see me?" West asked.

"Later," Chee said. He hurried out, the grin fading as his thoughts took better shape, and climbed into his pickup truck. The notebook was on the seat. He opened it, flipped to the proper page.

Across from "Why the burglary?" he wrote: "Was there a burglary?" Then he studied the other questions. Across from "Did Musket kill John Doe?" he wrote: "Was John Doe Ironfingers?" Then he closed the notebook, started the engine, and pulled the truck out of the trading post parking lot. He would talk to West later. First, he wanted time to think this through. Had West, the magician, the sorcerer, used Jim Chee to create one of his illusions? He wanted time to answer that. But now, as he drove down the bumpy road beside Wepo Wash, toward the reddish sunset, and the towering thunderclouds which promised rain and delivered nothing, he was fairly sure that when he had thought it through he would know the answer. The answer would be yes. Yes, for all these weeks Ironfingers had been hidden behind Jim Chee's stupidity.

25

◆

In fact, the answer was not a definite yes. It was "probably."

With sundown, the thunderheads lost their will to grow. With the cool darkness, they lost their will to live. Chee drove slowly, arm rested on the sill of the open truck window, enjoying the breeze. Lightning still flashed yellow and white in the cloud west of him, and the dark north also produced an occasional jagged bolt. But the clouds were dying. Overhead, the stars were out. The Colorado Plateau and the Painted Desert would live with drought through another cycle of sun. But Chee was aware of this only on a secondary level. He was reaching conclusions.

The man he'd seen coming from West's office; the man West had said he'd just fired; the man West said was Joseph Musket, might not have been Musket at all. Probably wasn't, Chee thought. West had simply used Jim Chee, a brand-new policeman who'd never seen Musket, to establish on the official record that Musket was alive, and well, and being fired by West, the day after John Doe's remains had been collected on Black Mesa. He'd done it neatly, asking Chee to come in when he knew some appropriate Navajo would be available, then arousing Chee's interest in the man when it was too late to get a good look at him. The pseudo Musket, Chee guessed, would be someone from somewhere else—whom Chee wouldn't be seeing around Burnt Water.

That was the first conclusion. The second revolved around

another illusion. West had probably performed his Musket deception, and then staged the pretended burglary, because Joseph Musket was already dead. Killed by whom? Probably by West himself. Why? Chee would leave that for later. There'd be a reason. There always was. Now he concentrated on the faded white line illuminated by his headlights, and on recreating what must have happened.

The cool air smelled of wet sage, and creosote bush, and ozone. For the first time in days, Chee felt in harmony with his thoughts. *Hozro* again. His mind was working as it should, on the natural path. West had found himself with the body of Musket on his hands. He had killed Musket, or someone else had done it, or Musket had simply died. And West didn't want it known. Not yet. Perhaps he'd gotten wind of the impending drug shipment. Perhaps his son had told him. Perhaps he'd learned it from Musket. And West wanted to steal it. And if shippers knew their man at Burnt Water was dead, they might move the landing point, or call everything off. So the death and the body had been concealed.

Chee found himself appreciating the cleverness. West knew he was dealing with very dangerous men. He knew they'd come after the thief. He wanted someone besides West for them to hunt. Ironfingers got the job. Which meant he could never, ever, afford the risk of having the corpse, or even the skeleton, of anyone who met Musket's description turning up to be identified. A skeleton, even a bit of jawbone, would be enough to match against the name of a missing person who'd been in prison—whose dental charts and fingerprints and all other vital statistics would be easily available. Therefore West had put the body out along the traditional pathway of the spruce Messenger's party, where it would be found exactly when he wanted it found. He'd faked the witchcraft mutilation—the hands and feet and probably the penis, too—to eliminate the automatic fingerprinting an unidentified corpse would undergo. It was his only wrong guess—not calculating that the Hopis wouldn't report the corpse before their Niman Kachina ceremonials—and it hadn't mattered. And then—Chee grinned again, savoring the cleverness of it—West had made certain that the official record would show Musket alive and well in Burnt Water after the corpse was found. That would kill any chance of matching dental charts. He would have done that, somehow, even if the body had been reported immediately.

Chee had this sorted out by the time his pickup made the long climb up the cliff of Moenkopi Wash, passed the Hopi village, and reached the Tuba City junction. By the time he'd reached Tuba City he reached another conclusion. West was hiding the body of Palanzer for the same reason he'd made Musket forever invisible. Palanzer-plus-Musket gave the owners of the cocaine an even more logical target for their rage.

Puddles from a rain do not long survive in a desert climate. The puddles in the track to Chee's mobile home had disappeared long ago. But the ruts were still soft and driving through them would cut them deeper. Chee parked the pickup, climbed out, and began walking the last fifty yards toward his home. There was still an occasional mutter of thunder from the north, but the sky now was a blaze of stars. Chee walked on the bunch grass, thinking that much of his problem still remained. There was absolutely nothing he could prove. All he would have for Captain Largo would be speculation. No. That wasn't true. Now the remains of John Doe could be identified—unless, of course, Musket had never been to a dentist. That wasn't likely. Chee enjoyed the night, the washed-clean smell of the air. The smell, suddenly, of brewing coffee.

Chee stopped in his tracks. Coffee! From where? He stared at his trailer. Dark and silent. It was the only possible source of that rich aroma. He had placed the trailer here under this lonely cottonwood for privacy and isolation. The site gave him that. The nearest other possible coffeepot was a quarter mile away. Someone was waiting in his dark trailer. They'd grown impatient. In the darkness, they'd brewed coffee. Chee turned and walked rapidly back toward his truck. The trailer produced a sudden clatter of sound. They'd been watching since he'd driven up and parked. They'd seen him turn away. Chee's walk became a run. He had his ignition key in his hand by the time he jerked the pickup door open. He heard the trailer door bang open, the sound of running feet. Then he had the key in the ignition. The still-warm motor roared into life. Chee slammed the gears into reverse, flicked on the headlights.

The lights illuminated two running men. One of them was the younger of the two men Chee had noticed watching him in the Hopi Cultural Center dining room. The other man Chee had seen hunting at the crash site, helping Johnson in his search for the suitcases. The younger man had a pistol in his hand. Chee switched off the lights and sent the pickup truck roaring backward down the track. He didn't turn on the headlights again until he was back on the asphalt.

26

◆

Chee spent the night beside his pickup truck in a sand-bottomed cul-de-sac off Moenkopi Wash. He'd stopped twice to make absolutely sure he hadn't been followed. Even so, he was nervous. He shaped the sand to fit hips and shoulders, rolled out his blanket, and lay looking up at a star-lit sky. Nothing remained of the afternoon's empty promise of rain except an occasional distant thunder from somewhere up around the Utah border. Why had the two men waited for him in his trailer? Obviously it hadn't been a friendly visit. Could he have been wrong about one of the men having been with Johnson in Wepo Wash? It would have made more sense for them to be members of the narcotics company. As Johnson had warned him, they might logically come looking for him. But why now? They would have learned by now that the dope was being sold back to them. Did they think that he was one of the hijackers doing the selling? He, and Musket, and Palanzer? But if the man had been the one he'd seen with Johnson in the wash, that meant something different. What would the DEA want with Chee? And why would the DEA wait for him in the dark, instead of calling him into Largo's office for a talk? Was it because, once again, the DEA's intentions were not wholly orthodox? Because he hadn't returned Johnson's call? That line of speculation led Chee nowhere. He turned his thoughts to the telephone call to Gaines. Tomorrow night the exchange would be made—five hundred thousand dollars in currency for two suitcases filled with cocaine. But where? All he knew now, that he hadn't known, was that the caller might have been West, and that Musket might be dead. That didn't seem to help. Then, as he thought it through all the way, through from the east, the south, the west, and the north, and back to the east again, just as his uncle had taught him, he saw that it might help. Everything must have a reason. Nothing was done without a cause. Why delay the payoff more than necessary—as the caller had done? How would tomorrow night be different from tonight? Different for West? Probably, somehow or other, the nights would be different on the Hopi ceremonial calendar. And West would be aware of the difference. He had been married to a Hopi. In the Hopi tradition, he had moved into the matriarchy of his wife—into her village and into her home. Three or four years, Dashee had said. Certainly long enough to know something of the Hopi religious calendar.

Chee shifted into a more comfortable position. The nervous tension was draining away now, the sense of being hunted. He felt relaxed and drowsy. Tomorrow he would get in touch with Dashee and find out what would be going on tomorrow night in the Hopi world of kachina spirits and men who wore sacred masks to impersonate them.

Chee was thinking of kachinas when he drifted off into sleep, and he dreamed of them. He awoke feeling stiff and sore. Shaking the sand out of his blanket, he folded it behind the pickup seat. Whoever had been waiting in his trailer had probably long since left Tuba City, but Chee decided not to take any chances. He drove southward instead, to Cameron. He got to the roadside diner just at sunrise, ordered pancakes and sausage for breakfast, and called Dashee from the pay telephone booth.

"What time is it?" Dashee said.

"It's late," Chee said. "I need some information. What's going on tonight at Hopi?"

"My God," Dashee shouted. "It's only a little after six. I just got to bed. I'm on the night shift for the next week."

"Sorry," Chee said. "But tell me about tonight."

"Tonight?" Dashee said. "There's nothing tonight. The Chu'tiwa—the Snake Dance ceremony—that's at Walpi day after tomorrow. Nothing tonight."

"Nowhere?" Chee asked. "Not in Walpi, or Hotevilla, or Bacobi, or anywhere?" He was disappointed and his voice showed it.

"Nothing much," Dashee said. "Just mostly stuff in the kivas. Getting ready for the Snake ceremonials. Private stuff."

"How about that village where West lived? His wife's village. Which one was it?"

"Sityatki," Dashee said.

"Anything going on there?"

There was a long pause.

"Cowboy? You still there?"

"Yeah," Cowboy said.

"Anything at Sityatki tonight?"

"Nothing much," Cowboy said.

"But something?"

"Nothing for tourists," Dashee said.

"What is it?"

"Well, it's something we call Astotokaya. It means Washing of the Hair. It's private. Sort of an initiation ceremony into the religious societies of the village."

It didn't sound to Chee like the sort of thing that would be useful to West.

"Does it draw a big crowd? I think that's what we're looking for."

Dashee laughed. "Just the opposite—they close the roads.

178

Nobody is supposed to come in. Everybody is supposed to stay indoors, not even look out the windows. People who live in houses that look out on the kivas, they move out. Nobody stirs except the people working on the initiation in the kivas and the young people getting initiated. And they don't come out until dawn."

"Tell me about it," Chee said. The disappointment was gone. He thought he knew, now, where West would set up his rendezvous.

Cowboy was reluctant. "It's confidential," he said. "Some of that stuff we're not really supposed to talk about."

"I think it might be important," Chee said. "A funny thing happened yesterday. I was at the cultural center, and the clerk got called away from the desk, and the telephone was ringing, so Miss Pauling went over there and worked the switchboard and—"

"I heard about that fire," Dashee said. "You start that fire?"

"Why would I start a fire?" Chee asked. "What I'm trying to tell you is Miss Pauling overheard this guy telling Gaines that the people who owned the cocaine could buy it back for five hundred thousand dollars. He said they should have the money available in two briefcases by nine o'clock Friday night. And he said he'd be back in touch to say where the trade-off would be made."

"How'd you know when to start the fire?" Dashee said. "How'd you know when that call was coming? You son of a bitch, you almost burned down the cultural center."

"The point is why hold off until nine o'clock Friday night? That's the question; and I think the answer is because they want to make the switch in a place where the buyers will figure there's going to be a bunch of curious people standing around watching, when actually it will be private."

"Sityatki," Cowboy said.

"Right. It makes sense."

Long pause, while Cowboy thought about it. "Not much," he said. "Why go to all that trouble if they're just going to swap money for cocaine?"

"Safety," Chee said. "They need to be someplace where the guys buying the dope back won't just shoot them and keep the money and everything."

"No safer there than anyplace else," Dashee argued.

Maybe it wasn't, Chee thought. But why else wait until nine Friday night? "Well," he said, "I think the swap's going to be made in Sityatki, and if you'd tell me more about what goes on, maybe I'll know why."

So Cowboy told him, reluctantly and haltingly enough so that Chee's pancakes and sausages were cold by the time he had prodded it all out, and it added nothing much. The crux of the matter was the village was sealed from darkness until dawn, people were supposed to remain indoors and not be looking out to spy on the spirits who visited the kivas during the night, and the place was periodically patrolled by priests of the kiva—but more ceremonially than seriously, Cowboy thought.

Chee took his time over breakfast, killing some of the minutes that had to pass before he could call Captain Largo at his office. Largo would be just a little bit late, and Chee wanted his call to be hanging there waiting for the captain when he walked in. Sometimes little psychological edges like that helped, and Chee was sure he'd need some.

"He's not in yet," the girl on the switchboard reported.

"You're sure?" Chee asked. "Usually he gets in about eight-oh-five."

"Just a minute," she amended. "He's driving into the parking lot."

Which was exactly how Chee had planned it.

"Largo," Largo said.

"This is Chee. There's a couple of things I have to report."

"On the telephone?"

"When I came in last night, there were two men waiting for me in my trailer. With the lights off. With a gun. One of them, anyway."

"Last night?" Largo said.

"About ten, maybe."

"And now you're reporting it?"

"I think one of them was Drug Enforcement. At least, I think I've seen him with Johnson. And if one was, I guess they both were. Anyway, I wasn't sure what to do, so I took off."

"Any violence?"

"No. I figured they were in there, so I headed back to my truck. They heard me and came running out. One of them had a gun, but no shooting."

"How'd you know they were there?"

"Smelled coffee," Chee said.

Largo didn't comment on that. "Those sons-a-bitches," he said.

"The other thing is that Miss Pauling told me she overheard a telephone call from some man to Gaines. He told Gaines he could have the cocaine back for five hundred thousand dollars and to be ready with the money at nine P.M. Friday and—"

"Where?"

"He didn't say. This isn't our case, so I didn't ask too many questions. I told Cowboy Dashee and I guess they'll go out and talk to her."

"Heard they had a little fire out there," Largo said. "You know anything about that?"

"I'm the one who reported it," Chee said. "Bunch of tumbleweeds caught on fire."

"Listen," Largo said. "I'm going to do some seeing about the way the DEA is behaving. We're not going to put up with any more of that. And when I talk to people I'm going to tell them that I gave you strict orders to stay away from this drug case. I'm going to tell people I'm going to kick your ass right out of the Navajo Police if I hear just one little hint that you're screwing around in federal territory. I'm going to tell people you understand that perfectly. That you know I'll do it. No question about it. You know that if you get anywhere near that drug case, or anybody involved with it, you are instantly and permanently suspended. Fired. Out of work."

Largo paused, allowing time for the speech to penetrate. "Now," he continued. "You do understand that, don't you? You understand that when I hang up this telephone I am going to write a memo for the files which will show that for the third and final time Jim Chee was officially and formally notified that any involvement on his part in this investigation would result in his immediate termination, said memo also showing that Chee did understand and agree to these instructions. Now, you got all that?"

"I got it," Chee said. "Just one thing, though. Would you put in the memo what I'm supposed to be doing? Put down that you've assigned me to working on that windmill, and solving the Burnt Water burglary, and finding Joseph Musket, and identifying that John Doe case up on Black Mesa. Would you put all that down, too?"

Another long pause. Chee guessed that Largo had never intended to write any memo for the record. Now he was examining Chee's motives.

"Why?" Largo asked.

"Just to get it all in, all in one place on the record."

"Okay," Largo said.

"And I think we should ask the medical examiner's office in Flagstaff to check the New Mexico State Penitentiary and see if they can come up with any dental x-rays on Joseph Musket, and then check them against the x-rays they took of John Doe's teeth."

"Wait a minute," Largo said. "You saw Musket alive after Doe's body was found."

"I saw somebody," Chee said. "West said it was Musket."

Another silence. "Ah," Largo said. "Yes, indeed."

"And about the windmill. I think I know who has been doing it, but it's nothing we're ever going to prove." He told Largo about the spring, and the shrine, and about how old Taylor Sawkatewa had tacitly admitted being there the night the plane had crashed, when Deputy Sheriff Dashee and Chee had talked to him.

"Wait a minute," Largo said. "When was this visit? It was after I ordered you to stay away from that drug case."

"I was working on the windmill," Chee said. "Sometimes you get more than you go after."

"I notice you do," Largo said grimly. "I've got to have the paperwork done on all this."

"Is tomorrow soon enough?"

"Just barely," Largo said. "What's wrong with coming in to work and doing it now?"

"I'm way down at Cameron," Chee said. "And I thought I'd spend the day seeing if I can catch us that Burnt Water burglar."

27

The first step toward what Chee called catching the Burnt Water burglar was ceremonial. In effect, Chee was going hunting. From their very beginnings, the Navajos had been a society of hunters. Like all hunting cultures, they approached the bloody, dangerous, and psychologically wounding business of killing one's fellow beings with elaborate care. Everything was done to minimize damage. The system had been devised in the dim, cold past, when the Dinees preyed with the wolves on the moose and caribou of the Arctic. And the first step of this system was the purification of the hunter.

There was no place anywhere near his trailer lot where Chee could build a sweat house. So he had found a place on the ridge behind Tuba City. He'd built it in a little arroyo, using one of the banks for a wall and erecting a sort of lean-to of rocks and juniper limbs. There was plenty of dead wood all around to fuel its fire pit. The necessary water Chee carried in from his truck in two collapsible plastic containers. By midmorning, the rocks were hot enough. Chee stripped to his Jockey shorts. He stood, facing east, and sang the first of the four sweat lodge songs:

"I am come from Graystreak Mountain;
I am standing nearby.
I am the Talking God,

A son of Female Wind. I stand near you
With a black bow in my right hand,
With a yellow-feathered arrow in my left hand.
I am the Talking God, standing ready. . . ."

He sang all the verses, dropped to his hands and knees, and ducked through the sweat house entrance into the hot darkness inside. He poured water from one of the plastic containers onto the sizzling boulders and pulled the heavy canvas cover down over the entrance. In the steamy blackness he sang three other songs, recounting how Talking God and the other *yei* figures of this legend had caught Black God in his guise as a crow, and how Black God had removed his suit of black feathers, and how Black God had been tricked, finally, into releasing all the game animals which he had held captive.

With that ritual finished, Chee was not certain how he should proceed. It was not the sort of question he would have ever thought to ask Frank Sam Nakai. "How, Uncle, does one prepare himself for a hunt which will take him into a Hopi village on a Holy Night when the kachina spirits are out? How does one prepare himself to trap another man?" Had he ever asked, he knew Frank Sam Nakai would have had an answer. He would have lit a cigaret, and smoked it, and finally he would have had an answer. Chee, his sweat bath songs finished, sat in the choking wet heat and thought about it in the Navajo Way—from east through north. The purpose of the hunting ceremony—the Stalking Way—was to put hunter and prey in harmony. If one was to hunt deer, the Stalking Way repeated the ancient formula by which man regained his ability to be one with the deer. One changed the formula only slightly to fit the animal. The animal, now, was man. An Anglo-American, ex-husband of a Hopi woman, trader with the Navajos, magician, wise, shrewd, dangerous. Chee felt the sweat pouring out of him, dripping from his chin and eyebrows and arms, and thought how to change the song to fit it to West. He sang:

"I am the Talking God. The Talking God,
I am going after him.
Below the east, I am going after him.
To that place in Wepo Wash, I am going after him.
I, being the Talking God, go in pursuit of him.
To Black Mesa, to the Hopi villages,
The chase will take me.
I am the Talking God. His luck will be with me.
His thoughts will be my thoughts as I go after him."

Verse after verse he sang, adopting the ancient ceremonial songs to meet this new need. The songs invoked Talking God, and Begochidi, and Calling God, and Black God himself, and the Predator People: First Wolf, First Puma, First Badger; recounting the role of Game Maker, and all the other Holy People of the Great Navajo myth of how hunting began and how man became himself a predator. Through it all, verse by verse, the purpose was the same as it had been since his ancestors hunted along the glaciers: to cross the prehuman flux and once again be as one with the hunted animal, sharing his spirit, his ways, thoughts, his very being.

Chee simply substituted "the man West" for "the fine buck" and sang on.

"In the evening twilight, the man West is calling to me.
Out of the darkness, the man West comes toward me.
Our minds are one mind, the man West and I, the Talking God.
Our Spirits are one spirit, the man West and I, the Talking God.
Toward my feathered arrow, the man West walks directly.

186

Toward my feathered arrow, the man West turns his
  side.
That my black bow will bless him with its beauty.
That my feathered arrow will make him like the Talking
  God.
That he may walk, and I may walk, forever in Beauty.
That we may walk with beauty all around us.
That my feathered arrow may end it all in Beauty."

There should be a final ceremony, and a final verse. In
the old, traditional days, the bow of the hunter would have
been blessed. These days, sometimes it was done to the rifle
before a deer hunt. Chee unsnapped his holster and extracted his pistol. It was a medium-barrel Ruger .38. He
was not particularly good with it, making his qualifying score
each year with very little to spare. He had never shot at
any living thing with it, and had never really decided what
he would do if the situation demanded that some fellow
human be fired upon. Given proper need, or proper provoca-
tion, Chee presumed he would shoot, but it wasn't the sort
of decision to be made in the abstract. Now Chee stared
at the pistol, trying to imagine himself shooting West. It
didn't work. He put the pistol back in the holster. As he
did, it occurred to him that the final verse of the usual sweat
bath ceremonial could not be done now. The prescribed
verse was the Blessing Song from the Blessing Way. But
Jim Chee, a shaman of the Slow Talking People, could sing
no blessing songs now. Not until this hunt was finished and
he had returned to this sweat bath to purify himself again.
Until then, Jim Chee had turned himself into a predator,
dedicated by the Stalking Way songs to the hunt. The Blessing Song would have to wait. It put one in harmony with
beauty. The Stalking Way put one in harmony with death.

28

◆

Jim Chee waited for West, or for Ironfingers, or for whoever would come, just as a mountain lion waits for game at a watering place. He picked a place which gave him a good view of the burial place of the suitcases and from which he could move quickly to make an arrest. He had checked the area and found no sign that West's jeep, or any other vehicle, had been here since Johnson's futile search. He poked his jack handle into the sand until he felt the steel tapping against aluminum. The bait was still in place. Then he sat behind a screen of junipers on the bank of the wash and waited. He didn't expect West to come. But if West did come, Chee would be waiting.

It was midafternoon now, a little less than six hours before the 9:00 P.M. deadline the caller had announced for the transfer of drugs for money. It was humid—a rare circumstance for the Colorado plateau—and the thunderheads were boiling up northward toward Utah and over the Mogollon Rim to the West. Chee still felt the effects of the heat and dehydration of the sweat bath. He'd taken two huge drinks of water to replace the lost fluids and was, in fact, sweating again now. Still, he felt a kind of clear, clean sharpness in his vision and in his mind. Hosteen Nakai had taught him of the time when all intelligent things were still in flux, when what-would-be-animal and that-which-would-be-human could still talk together, and change forms. In a ceremonial way, the Stalking Way was intended to restore that ancient power on some much-limited intellectual level. Chee wondered about it as he waited. Was he seeing and thinking a little more like a wolf or a puma?

There was no way to answer that. So he reviewed all he knew of this affair, from the very beginning, concentrating on West. West the magician, causing him to think of mental telepathy instead of the mathematics of how a deck of cards can be divided. West misdirecting the attention of the Navajo buying the rope, misdirecting Chee's attention away from the easy solution of the three of diamonds, misdirecting attention away from why Joseph Musket's hands were flayed. Always distorting reality with illusion. And now, why was West asking only five hundred thousand dollars for a cocaine shipment that the DEA said was worth many millions of dollars? Why so little? Because he wanted it fast? Because he wanted to minimize any risk that the owners wouldn't be willing to buy it back? Because West was not a greedy man? That was his reputation. And it seemed to be justified. He had no expensive tastes. No drinking. No women. As trading posts went, Burnt Water seemed to be moderately profitable, and West's prices, and his interest rate on pawn, showed no tendency to gouge. He was, in fact, known to be generous on occasion. Cowboy had told him once of West giving a drunk twenty dollars for bus fare to Flagstaff. Not the act of a man who valued money for money's sake.

So what would he do with five hundred thousand dollars? How would he use it, a lonely man with no one to spend it on, no one to spend it with? There must be a reason for demanding it, for setting up the steal, for the killing and the danger. A West reason. A white man's reason.

Chee stared out across the sandy bottom of Wepo Wash. Slowly, the white man's reason emerged. Chee checked it against everything he knew, everything that had happened. Everywhere it fit. Now he was sure West wouldn't come for the suitcases.

Chee left his hiding place, and walked back to the arroyo where he had left his patrol car. He drove it, with no effort at all at concealment, up the wash to the crash location. He parked it beside the basalt upthrust. His shovel was in his pickup truck but he didn't really need it. He dug with his hands, exposing the two suitcases, and pulled them out. They were surprisingly heavy—each sixty to seventy pounds, he guessed. He loaded them into the trunk of his patrol car, slammed the trunk shut, then reached in through the window and got his clipboard.

If he was right, this work was wasted. But if he was wrong, someone would come today—or someday—to dig up the cache and vanish with it. Questions would be left unanswered then, and Chee would no longer have a way to find the answers. Chee hated unanswered questions.

On the notepad on the clipboard, he wrote in block print: I HAVE THE SUITCASES. HANG AROUND BURNT WATER AND REMEMBER THE NUMBER OF LETTERS IN THIS MESSAGE. Then he counted the letters. Seventy-nine.

He fished through the glove box, found an empty aspirin bottle he used to keep matches in, removed the matches, and folded in the note. He wiped off his fingerprints and dropped the bottle in the hole where the suitcases had been.

29

◆

The village of Sityatki, like many of the Southwest's pueblo villages, had been split by the human lust for running water. The original village still perched atop the east cliff of Third Mesa, from which it stared four hundred feet straight down into the sandy bottom of Polacca Wash. But along the wash itself, the Bureau of Indian Affairs had built a scattering of those brown frame-and-plaster bungalows which are standard government housing, equipped them with refrigerators and a pressure-tank water system, and thereby lured perhaps three-fourths of the younger residents of Sityatki down from the cliffs. The deserters, for the most part, remained loyal to village traditions, to their duties to the Fox, Coyote, and Fire clans which had founded it in the fourteenth century, and to the religious society into which they had been initiated. But they were usually present in the village only in spirit, and when ceremonial occasions required. Tonight, the presence of most of them was not required—was in fact discouraged—and the little stone houses which were theirs by right through the wombs of their mothers and grandmothers and great-grandmothers for twenty or so generations now stood empty. Tonight was the night of the Washing of the Hair, when the four great religious fraternities of the village—the Wuchim, the Flute, the One Horn, the Two Horn—initiate young people. For more than a week, the *na'chi* of the Wuchim Society had been planted atop the

191

Wuchim kiva at the east edge of the Sityatki plaza, its sparrow-hawk feathers ruffled by the August breezes—a sort of flag notifying the Hopis that the priests of Wuchim were preparing for the ritual. The kivas of the three other societies were also marked by their distinctive standards. And this afternoon the few families who still lived on the east side of the village had moved from their houses and hung blankets over windows and doorways. When darkness came, no profane eyes would be looking out to witness the kachinas coming from the spirit world to visit the kivas and bless their new brothers.

Jim Chee knew this—or thought he knew it—because he had taken a course in Southwestern ethnology at UNM, which had taught him enough to pry a little more out of a reluctant and uneasy Cowboy Dashee.

Chee had never been to Sityatki, but he'd had Cowboy describe it in wearisome (for Cowboy) detail—from the layout of its streets to the ins and outs of its single dead-ended access road. Now he reached one of the few "outs" the road offered, a side track which zigzagged downward to provide risky access to the bottom of Polacca Wash. His plan was to leave the car here, out of sight from the access road. If what Dashee had told him was accurate, a little after dark a priest of the One Horn Society would emerge from the society's kiva and "close" the road by sprinkling a line of corn meal and pollen across it. He would then draw similar sacred lines across the footpaths leading into the village from the other directions, barring entry except by the "spirit path" used by the kachinas. Chee's intentions were to reach the village when it was dark enough to avoid being seen by West, or anyone else who might know him, but before Sityatki was ceremonially closed against intruders. Chee parked the car behind a growth of junipers near the wash, transferred the flashlight from the glove box to the hip pocket of his jeans, and locked the door. About a mile to walk, he guessed, including the steep climb back up to the mesa rim. But he'd left himself at least an hour of daylight. Plenty of time.

He hadn't covered a hundred yards when he saw West's jeep. Like Chee's patrol car, it had been driven behind a screen of brush. Chee checked it quickly, saw nothing interesting, and hurried up the hill. He felt a sense of urgency. Why had West come so early? Probably for the same reason that had motivated Chee. He had probably called in the location of the meeting place at the last possible moment and then rushed to make sure he'd be here first and that no trap could be set for him. On the mesa top, Chee kept away from the road but near enough to watch it. An old pickup passed, driving a little faster than the bumpy road made wise or comfortable. Hopis, Chee guessed, hurrying to some ceremonial duty, or perhaps just anxious to get to their homes before the village was sealed. Then came a car, dark blue and new, a Lincoln edging cautiously over the stony surface. Chee stopped and watched it, feeling excitement rising. It wouldn't be a local car. It might be a sightseer, but the usually hospitable Hopis did not advertise this event, nor encourage tourists to come to it. More likely, the blue Lincoln confirmed his guess about where West had arranged the buy-back. This was The Boss coming to ransom his cocaine shipment. The car eased into a depression, moving at no more than walking speed. At the bottom of the dip, the rear door opened, and a crouching man stepped out, clicked the door shut behind him, and was out of sight behind the junipers along the cliff. Too much distance, too little light, too short a moment for Chee to register whether the man looked familiar. He could see only that he was blond, and wore a blue-and-gray shirt. The Boss apparently had not followed orders to come alone; he'd brought along a bodyguard. Like Chee, the bodyguard intended to slip into the village unnoticed.

193

Chee waited; he wanted to give this man time to get well ahead. But when he thought of it, it didn't matter whether this fellow saw him or not. Out of uniform, in his off-day jeans and work shirt, Chee conceded that he would be seen by this white man as just another Hopi walking home from wherever he'd been. Chee conceded this reluctantly. To Chee, Navajos and Hopis, or Navajos and anyone else for that matter, looked no more alike than apples and oranges. It wasn't until Hosteen Nakai pointed out to him that after three years at the University of New Mexico, Chee still couldn't sort out Swedes from Englishmen, or Jews from Lebanese, that Chee was willing to admit that this "all Indians look alike" business with white men was genuine, something to be added to his growing store of data about the Anglo-American culture.

Chee hurried again, not worrying about being seen. Like himself, the man who had slipped out of the car was keeping away from the road. And like Chee, he was skirting along the rim of the mesa. Chee kept him periodically in sight for a while, and then lost him as the twilight deepened. He didn't think it would matter. Sityatki was a small place— a cluster of no more than fifty residences crowded around two small plazas, each with two small kivas. It shouldn't be hard to find the blue Lincoln.

He reached the edge of the village a little earlier than he'd planned. The sun was well below the horizon now, but the clouds which had been building up all afternoon gave the dying light a sort of glum grayness. Far to the west, back over the Mogollon Rim and Grand Canyon country, the sky was black with storm. Chee stopped beside a plank outhouse, glanced at his watch, and decided to wait for a little more darkness. No breeze moved the air. It was motionless and, rarity of rarities in this climate, damp with a warm, smothering humidity. Maybe it would rain. Really rain—a soaking, drought-breaking deluge. Chee hoped it would, but he didn't expect it. Even when the storm is breaking, the desert dweller maintains his inbred skepticism about clouds. He finds it hard to believe in rain even when it's falling on him. He's seen too many showers evaporate between thunderclap and the parched earth.

There was thunder now, a distant boom, which echoed from somewhere back over Black Mesa. And when it died away, Chee heard a faint, rhythmic sound. Ceremonial drumming, he guessed, from the depth of one of the village kivas. It would be time to move.

A path from the outhouse led along the rim of the cliff, skirting past the outermost wall of the outermost residence, threading through a narrow gap between the uneven stones and open space. Chee took it. Far below, at the bottom of the wash, the darkness was almost total. Lights were on in the BIA housing—rectangles of bright yellow—and the headlights of a vehicle were moving slowly down the road which followed the dry watercourse. Normally Chee had no particular trouble with heights. But now he felt an uneasy, shaky nervousness. He moved along the wall, turned into the walkway between two of the crowded buildings, and found himself looking out into the plaza.

No one was in sight. Neither was the blue Lincoln. An old Plymouth, a flatbed truck, and a half-dozen pickups were parked here and there beside buildings on the north and west sides of the plaza, and an old Ford with its rear wheels removed squatted unevenly just beside where Chee stood.

The black belly of the cloud beyond the village lit itself with internal lightning, flashed again, and then faded back into black. From the kiva to his left, Chee heard the sound of drumming again and muffled voices raised in rhythmic chanting. The cloud responded to the call with a bumping roll of thunder. Where could the Lincoln be?

Chee skirted the plaza, keeping close to the buildings and making himself as unobtrusive as possible, remembering what Dashee had told him of the layout of this village. He found the alley which led to the lower plaza, a dark tunnel between rough stone walls. Across the lower plaza, the blue Lincoln was parked.

The oldest part of the village surrounded this small open space, and much of it had been deserted generations ago. From where Chee stood in the blackness of the alley mouth, it appeared that only two of the houses might still be in use. The windows of one glowed with a dim yellow light and the other, two doorways down, was producing smoke from its stovepipe chimney. Otherwise there was no sign of life. The window frames had been removed from the house against which Chee leaned and part of its roof had fallen in. Chee peered into the dark interior and then stepped over the windowsill onto the packed-earth floor inside. As he did so, he heard a rattling sound. It approached, suddenly louder. Rattle. Rattle. Rattle. The sounds were spaced as if someone, walking slowly, shook a rattle with each step. The sound was in the alley which Chee had just left. And then Chee saw a shape move past the window he had just stepped through.

A booming rumble of thunder drowned out the sound. Under cover of the noise Chee moved cautiously to the front of the building, ducking under fallen roof beams. Through the hole where the front door had been, he could see the walking man slowly circling the little plaza. He wore a ceremonial kirtle, which came to about his knees. Rattles made of tortoise shells were tied just below his knees. On his head he wore a sort of helmet, dominated by two great horns, curved like the horns of a ram. In his hand he carried what looked like a staff. As Chee watched, the walker stopped.

He turned, and faced Chee.

"*Haquimi?*" The walker shouted the question directly toward him.

Chee froze, held his breath. The man couldn't possibly see him. There was still a residue of twilight in the plaza, but the darkness under this fallen roof was complete. The walker pivoted, with a flourish of his rattles, and faced a quarter turn away from Chee's hiding place. *"Haquimi?"* he shouted again, and again he stood motionless, waiting for an answer that didn't come. Another quarter turn, and again the question was shouted. Chee relaxed. This would be part of the patrol Cowboy had told him about—members of the One Horn and Two Horn societies giving their kivas the ceremonial assurance that they were safe from intruders. They shout "Who are you?" Cowboy had said, and of course nobody answers because nobody is supposed to be out except Masaw and certain of the kachinas, coming into the village over the spirit path. If there's a kachina coming, then he answers, "I am I."

The patrol was facing to Chee's left now. He shouted his question again. This time, instantly, it was answered. *"Pin u-u-u."* A hooting sound, more birdlike than human. It came from somewhere just off the little plaza, out of the darkness, and it made the hair bristle on Chee's neck. The voice of a kachina answering his human brother? Chee stared through the doorway, trying to place the sound. He heard the mutter of thunder and the cadenced rattles of the patrol, walking slowly away from the source of the response. A flare of lightning lit the plaza. It was empty.

Chee glanced at the luminous dial of his watch. The caller had said 9:00 P.M. for the transfer. Still almost an hour to wait. Why so long? West (or should he still be thinking of Ironfingers?) must have told the man in the blue Lincoln to arrive by twilight, before the road was closed. Must have told the man where to park, and to sit in his car and wait. But why so long? Why not get it over with? Lightning again—a great jagged bolt which struck somewhere back on Black Mesa. It lit the empty plaza with a brief white light, bright enough to show Chee that the man in the blue Lincoln was wearing a straw hat.

Chee was aware he was sweating. Unusual in desert country—especially unusual after dark, when temperatures tended to drop. Tonight the humidity held the day's heat like a damp blanket. Surely it would rain. Another flash of lightning, repeated and repeated. Chee saw that the house to the left of the alley he'd used was also empty and abandoned. It would give him a better view of the Lincoln. Under the cover of the booming thunder, he slipped from his hiding place, crossed the narrow passageway, and stepped through the empty window.

He stood a moment, giving his eyes a chance to adjust to the deeper darkness here. Something teased his nostrils. A sweetish smell. Faint. Somehow chemical. Like a bad perfume. Lightning. Far away, but producing enough brightness through the open doorway to show him he stood on the earth floor of an empty room. A room littered with scattered debris, fallen plaster, wind-blown trash. To his left, a gaping doorway into what must be a back room. The smell might come from there. But the smell could wait. He moved to the doorway. It gave him a good view of the Lincoln and he stood staring at the dark shape, waiting for lightning to show him more.

Suddenly there was a breeze, surprisingly cool, wet, and carrying the rich and joyful perfume of rain. The breeze died as abruptly as it had risen and Chee heard the rattle, rattle, rattle, of the ceremonial patrolman's tortoise shells. The sound was very close and Chee shrank back from the doorway. As he did, the patrolman walked slowly past. A different patrolman. Chee could see only a dark shape, but this man was larger. Lightning lit the plaza briefly and Chee saw the man was peering into the empty doorway of the adjoining house.

Chee moved as quickly as caution and the darkness would allow toward where his memory told him he'd seen the entrance to the back room. He'd be out of sight there, even if the patrolman checked this house. He moved his fingertips along the rough plaster, found the wooden doorframe, and moved through the opening, placing his feet cautiously in the darkness. The smell now was strong. A distinctly chemical smell. Chee frowned, trying to identify it. He moved carefully, back into the blackness. Then stopped. Within a few feet of him, someone breathed.

It was a low sound, the simple exhalation of a deep breath. Chee froze. A long way over the mesa, thunder thumped and rumbled and died away. Silence. And into the silence the faint sound of breath taken, breath exhaled. Easy, steady breathing. It seemed to come from the floor. Someone asleep? Chee took the flashlight from his back pocket, wrapped several thicknesses of his shirttail over the lens, squatted, pointed the light toward the sound. He flicked it on, and off again.

The dim light showed a small, elderly man sprawled on his back on the floor. The man wore only boxer shorts, a blue shirt, and moccasins. He seemed to be asleep. Still squatting, Chee edged two steps closer and flicked on the light again. The man wore his hair in the short bangs of old-fashioned Hopi traditionalists, and seemed to have some sort of ceremonial decoration painted on his forehead and cheeks. Where were his trousers? Chee risked the flashlight again. The room was bare. No sign of clothing. What was the man doing here? Drunk, most likely. In here to sleep it off.

Chee put the flashlight back in his pocket. From outside he heard the ceremonial question being called by the patrolman. He returned to the outer room. Still forty minutes to wait. It would be safe again to resume his watch of the Lincoln.

Chee stood just inside the exterior doorway. It was full night now, but the open plaza, even on this cloudy night, was much lighter than the interior from which Chee watched. He could see fairly well, and he saw the patrolman-priest of the Two Horn Society walking slowly toward the Lincoln. The priest stopped beside the car, standing next to the door where the man in the straw hat sat, leaning toward him. In the silence, Chee heard a voice, low and indistinct. Then another voice. The watchman asking straw hat what he was doing there? Or telling him to move? What would straw hat do? And why hadn't West, or whoever had set this up, foreseen this snag in their plans?

As that question occurred to him, Chee thought of the answer to an earlier question. Several earlier questions. The man in the back room wasn't drunk. He wouldn't be drunk on such a ceremonial occasion. The sweet chemical smell was chloroform. The man hadn't been wearing trousers. He'd been wearing a ceremonial kirtle. And tortoise shell rattles. He'd been knocked out, and stripped of his Two Horn costume.

At the blue Lincoln, the Two Horn priest was moving away from the car window now, moving fast. No longer did he rattle as he walked.

There was a blinding flash of blue-white light, followed almost instantly by an explosive crash of thunder. The flash illuminated the Two Horn priest. He was hurrying past the kiva toward a gap in the buildings which led to the upper plaza. He must be West. But he should have been carrying two briefcases. He should have been carrying five hundred thousand dollars. He was carrying nothing. Chee hesitated a moment and then sprinted to the Lincoln. The first drops struck him as he ran across the plaza. Huge, icy blobs of water, scattered at first, and then a cold, thunderous torrent.

Again there was lightning. A tall blond man emerged from a ruined building just beyond where the Lincoln was parked. He had something in his hand, perhaps a pistol. He was moving fast, like Chee, toward the car. The flash told Chee little more than that—just the blond man in the blue-and gray shirt and a glimpse of the Lincoln, where the hat was no longer visible.

The blond got to the car perhaps three seconds before Chee did. Chee didn't intend to stop—didn't have time to stop. The blue Lincoln, the straw hat, didn't concern Chee now. But the blond man stopped him.

He put up his left hand. "Help him," the blond man said. The rain was a downpour now. Chee extracted his flashlight, turned it on. The rain beat against the back of his head, streamed down the face of the blond man, who stood motionless, looking stunned. A pistol hung from his right hand, water dripping from it.

"Put away your gun," Chee said. He pulled open the front door of the Lincoln. The straw hat had fallen on the floorboards under the steering wheel and the middle-aged man who had worn it had fallen too, sideways, his head toward the passenger's side. In the yellow light of the flash, the blood that was pouring from his throat across the pale-blue upholstery looked black. Chee leaned into the car for a closer look. The damage seemed to have been done with something like a hunting knife. Mostly the throat, and the neck—at least a dozen savage slashing blows.

Chee backed out of the front seat.

"Help him," the blond man said.

"I can't help him," Chee said. "Nobody can help him. He killed him."

"That goddamned Indian," the blond man said. "Why did he?"

There were two briefcases on the floorboards on the passenger side. Blood was dripping off the front seat onto one of them. West could have taken them by simply reaching in and picking them up. He'd asked for five hundred thousand dollars. Why hadn't he taken it?

"It wasn't an Indian," Chee said. "And I don't know why."

But as he said it, he did know why. West wanted vengeance, not money. That's what all this had been about. The dark wind ruled Jake West. Chee left the blond man standing by the Lincoln and ran across the plaza. West would head for his jeep. He wouldn't know anyone knew where he'd parked it.

30

◆

The first leg of the trip to the place where West had left his jeep Chee covered at a run. That phase ended when he ran into a piñon limb, which knocked him off his feet and inscribed a bloody scratch across the side of his forehead. After that he alternated a fast walk, where visibility was bad, with a cautious trot, where it wasn't. The rain squall passed away to the east, the sky lightened a little, and Chee found himself doing more running than walking. He wanted to reach the jeep before West got there. He wanted to be waiting for West. But when he found the thickets where the jeep was parked, and pushed his way through them as quietly as he could, West was already climbing into the driver's seat.

Chee pulled out his pistol and flicked on the flash.

"Mr. West," he said. "Hold your hands up where I can see them."

"Who's that?" West said. He squinted into the brightness. "Is that you, Chee?"

Chee was remembering the bloody throat of the man in the Lincoln. "Get your hands up," he said. "That sound you hear is me cocking this pistol."

West raised his hands, slowly.

"Get out," Chee said.

West climbed out of the jeep.

"Put your hands on the hood. Spread your legs apart."

Chee searched him, removed a snub-nosed revolver from his hip pocket. He found nothing else. "Where's the knife?" he asked.

West said nothing.

"Why didn't you take the money?" Chee asked him.

"I wasn't after money," West said. "I wanted the man. And I got the son of a bitch."

"Because your son was killed?"

"That's right," West said.

"I think maybe you killed the wrong one," Chee said.

"No," West said. "I got the right one. The one who gave the orders."

"Put your hands behind your back," Chee said. He handcuffed West.

Chee was suddenly dazzled by a beam of light.

"Drop the gun," a voice ordered. "Now! Drop it!"

Chee dropped his pistol.

"And the flashlight!"

Chee dropped the flashlight. It produced a pool of light at his feet.

"You're a persistent bastard," the voice said. "I told you to stay away from this."

It was Johnson's voice. And it was Johnson's face Chee could see now in the reflected light. "Hands behind your back," he said, and cuffed Chee's hands behind him.

He picked up Chee's pistol, and West's, and tossed them into the back of West's jeep.

"Okey dokey," Johnson said. "Let's get this over with and get out of the rain. Let's go get the coke." He gestured with the pistol toward West. "Where've you got it?"

"I guess I'll get me a lawyer and talk to him first," West said.

Chee laughed, but he didn't feel like laughing. He felt stupid. He should have expected Johnson. Johnson would have found a way to intercept West's instructions about the meeting. Certainly if another telephone call was involved, tapping a line would be no problem for the DEA agent. "I don't think Johnson is going to read your rights to you," Chee said.

"No, I'm not," Johnson said. "I'm going to leave him with the same deal he made the organization. He keeps the five hundred thousand dollars. I get the coke."

"How do you know he hasn't already delivered it?" Chee asked.

"Because I've been watching him," Johnson said. "He hasn't picked the stuff up."

"But maybe he had it stashed out in the village up there," Chee said.

Johnson ignored him. "Come on," he said to West. "We'll take my car. We'll go get the stuff."

West didn't move. He stared through the flashlight beam at Johnson. Johnson hit him with the pistol—a smashing blow across the face. West staggered backward, lost his balance, fell against the jeep.

Johnson chuckled. There was lightning again, a series of flashes. The rain came down harder. "That surprised him," Johnson said to Chee. "He still thinks I'm your regular-type cop. You don't think that, do you?"

"No," Chee said. "I haven't thought that for a while."

West was trying to get to his feet, awkwardly because of his arms cuffed behind him. "Not since when?" Johnson asked. "I'm curious."

"Well," Chee said, "when you were hunting for the shipment down by the crash site, down in Wepo Wash, one of those guys hunting with you was one of the hoods. Or at least I thought he might be. But I was already suspicious."

"Because I knocked you around?"

West was on his feet now, blood running down his cheek. Chee delayed his answer a moment. He wanted to make sure West was listening to it.

"Because of the way you set up West's boy in the penitentiary. You take him away from the prison, and somehow or other you get him to talk, and then you put him back with the regular population. If you'd have put him in a segregation cell to keep him safe, then the organization would have known he'd talked. They'd have called off the delivery."

"That's fairly clear thinking," Johnson said. He laughed again. "You know for sure the son of a bitch is going to have to absolutely guarantee everybody that he didn't say one damn word."

In the yellow light of the flash, West's face was an immobile mask staring at Johnson.

"And you know for sure they're not going to let him stay alive, not with you maybe coming back to talk to him again," Chee said.

"I can't think of any reason to keep you around," Johnson said. "Can you think of one?"

Chee couldn't. He could only guess that Johnson was stalling just a little so that the shot that killed Chee would be covered by thunder. When the next flash of lightning came, Johnson would wait a moment until the thunderclap started, and then he would shoot Chee.

"I can think of a reason to kill you," Johnson said. "West, here, he'll see me do it and then he'll know for sure that I won't hesitate to do it to him if he don't cooperate."

"I can think of one reason not to kill me," Chee said. "I've got the cocaine."

Johnson grinned.

There was a flicker of lightning. Chee found himself hurrying.

"It's in two suitcases. Aluminum suitcases."

Johnson's grin faded.

"Now, how would I know that?" Chee asked him.

"You were out there when the plane crashed," Johnson said. "Maybe you saw West and Palanzer and that goddamn

206

crooked Musket unloading it and hauling it away."

"They didn't haul it away," Chee said. "West dug a hole in the sand behind that outcrop and put in the two suitcases and covered them over with sand and patted the sand down hard, and the next morning you federals walked all over the place and patted it down some more."

"Well, now," Johnson said.

"So I went out and took the jack handle out of my truck and did some poking around in the sand until I hit metal and then dug. Two aluminum suitcases. Big ones. Maybe thirty inches long. Heavy. Weight maybe seventy pounds each. And inside them, all these plastic packages. Pound or so each. How much would that much cocaine be worth?"

Johnson was grinning again, wolfishly. "You saw it," he said. "It's absolutely pure. Best in the world. White as snow. Fifteen million dollars. Maybe twenty, scarce like it is this year."

Lightning flashed. In a second it would thunder.

"So you've got a fifteen-million-dollar reason to keep me alive," Chee said.

"Where is it?" Johnson asked. Thunder almost drowned out the question.

"I think we better talk business first," Chee said.

"A little bit of larceny in everybody's heart," Johnson said. "Well, there's enough for everybody this time." He grinned again. "We'll take your car. Police radio might come in handy. If Mr. West here stirred up any trouble back there in the village, it'd be nice to know about it."

"My car?" Chee said.

"Don't get cute," Johnson said. "I saw it. Parked right down the slope in all those bushes. Let's go."

The rain was a downpour again now. The Navajos have terms for rain. The brief, noisy, violent thunderstorm is "male rain." The slower, enduring, soaking shower is "female rain." But they had no word for this kind of storm.

They walked through a deafening wall of falling water, breathing water, almost blinded by water. Johnson walked behind him, West stumbling dazedly in front, the beam of Johnson's flash illuminating only sheets of rain.

They stopped beside Chee's car.

"Get out your keys," Johnson said.

"Can't," Chee said. He had to shout over the pounding of rain on the car roof.

"Try," Johnson said. He had the pistol pointed at Chee's chest. "Try hard. Strain yourself. Otherwise I whack you on the head and get 'em out myself."

Chee strained. Twisting hips and shoulders, he managed to hook his trigger finger into his pants pocket. Then he pulled his trousers around an inch or two. He managed to fish out the key ring.

"Drop it and back off," Johnson said. He picked up the keys.

Chee became aware of a second sound, even louder than the pounding of the rain. Polacca Wash had turned into a torrent. This cloudburst had been developing over Black Mesa for an hour, moving slowly. Behind it and under it, millions of tons of water were draining off the mesa down dozens of smaller washes, scores of arroyos, ten thousand little drainage ways—all converging on Polacca, and Wepo, sending walls of water roaring southwestward to pour into the Little Colorado River. The roaring Chee could hear was the sound of brushwood and dislodged boulders rumbling down Polacca under the force of the flood. In two hours, there wouldn't be a bridge, or a culvert, or an uncut vehicle crossing between the Hopi Mesas and the river canyon.

Johnson was tossing the keys in his palm, staring thoughtfully at Chee and West. The flashlight beam bobbed up and down. In the light, Chee could see how much the flood had already risen. The turbulent water was tearing at the junipers no more than twenty-five feet down the slope from where he'd parked.

"I've just been having some interesting thoughts," Johnson said. "I think I know where you've got that cocaine."

"I doubt it," Chee said.

"I've been asking myself why you two guys didn't come together. You know, save gasoline, wear and tear on the tires. And I tell myself that West, he wanted to come early and scout things out to make sure nobody's got you set up. So he don't bring the cocaine. Where do you hide it in a jeep?"

As Johnson talked, he let the beam of the flash drift to the windows of Chee's patrol car. He looked inside.

"Then after West has everything scouted out and it's safe—and if anybody grabs him they gotta just turn him loose because he doesn't have the stuff and they want it—after all that, along comes Mr. Chee here in his police car. And what could be a safer place to hide cocaine than in a police car?"

Johnson shone the flash into Chee's eyes.

"Where's safer than that?" he insisted.

"Sounds great," Chee said. He was trying desperately to make some sort of plan. Johnson would open the trunk and look. Then there would be no reason at all to keep Chee alive. Or West alive. The flash left Chee's face and moved to West. Bloody water was streaming down from the cut across West's cheekbone, running into his beard. Chee thought he'd never seen so much hate in a face. West understood now why his son had died. West understood he'd knifed the wrong man.

"Sounds like a good little theory," Johnson said. "Let's see how it works out in real life."

He put the flash under his armpit and kept the pistol pointed at Chee while he fumbled with getting the key into the lock. The trunk lid sprang open. The trunk lights lit the scene.

Johnson laughed, a joyful chortle of a laugh.

"One little problem remains," Chee said. "What if what you see there are two suitcases containing Pillsbury's Best wheat flour. It doesn't weigh as much as the cocaine, but if you don't know how heavy those things are supposed to be, you could never tell the difference by looking."

"We'll just take a look, then," Johnson said. "I can tell the difference and I'm getting a little tired of you."

He put the flash in the trunk, kept the pistol aimed at Chee. He didn't look at the suitcases, but Chee could hear him fumbling with a catch.

"Where's the key?" he asked.

"I don't think they sent one along," Chee said. "Maybe they mailed the key to the buyers. Who knows?"

"Keep back," Johnson said. He pulled both suitcases upright, unfastened the tire tool, and jammed the screwdriver end into a joint. He pried. The lock snapped. The suitcase fell open. Johnson stared.

"Looky there," he chortled.

Chee moved, but West moved faster. Even so, Johnson had time to swing the pistol around and fire twice before West reached him. West was screaming—an incoherent animal shriek. Johnson tried to step away, slipped on the wet surface. West's shoulder slammed him against the open trunk. There was the sound of something breaking. Chee moved as fast as he could, off balance because of his pinned arms. The collision had knocked Johnson off his feet and West, too, had fallen. Chee stood with his hands in the trunk, fumbling for the tire tool, for anything his hands could grasp that he could use—hands behind him—to kill a man.

The unopened aluminum suitcase had been knocked on its side. His hands found its handle. He pulled it out of the trunk, staggering momentarily as the weight swung free. Johnson was regaining his feet now, feeling around him in the darkness for the fallen pistol.

Chee spun, swinging the suitcase behind him, guessing, releasing it at the point where he hoped it would hit Johnson. It missed.

The suitcase bounced just past Johnson's legs, and tumbled down the slope toward the roaring water of Polacca Wash.

"My God," Johnson screamed. He scrambled after it.

West was on his feet again now, running clumsily after Johnson. The rain pounded down. Lightning flashed, illuminating falling water with a blue-white glare.

The suitcase had stopped just above the water's edge, held by a juniper. Johnson had reached it and was pulling it to safety when he realized what West was doing. He turned and was struck by West's body, and went sprawling backward downhill into what was now Polacca River.

West was lying, head down, feet high, beside the suitcase. Chee struggled down the slope, slipping and sliding.

He sat beside West. "You all right?"

West was breathing hard. "Did I knock him in?"

"You got the right man this time," Chee said. "Nobody could swim in that water. He's drowning. Or by now, maybe he's drowned."

West said nothing. He simply breathed.

"Can you get up?"

"I can try," West said, He tried. A brief struggle. Then he lay still again. His breathing now had a bubble in it.

"You're going to have to get up," Chee said. "The water's rising and I can't help you much."

West struggled again. Chee managed to catch his arm and pull him upward. They got him on his knees, on his feet. Finally, after two falls, they got him to the car, and into it. They sat, side by side, under the overhead light, on the front seat, simply breathing. The rain pounded thunderously against the roof.

"I've got a problem," Chee said. "The key to the handcuffs I'm wearing is in Johnson's pocket and there's no way we're going to get that. But the key to the handcuffs on you is on my key ring. If I take off your cuffs, can you drive?"

West's breath bubbled in his chest. "Maybe," he said, very faintly.

"They're checking on Joseph Musket's dental charts," Chee said. "Comparing them with the John Doe the witch is supposed to have killed. They're going to match, so they're going to nail you for killing Musket."

"Worked pretty well, though," West said. He made a sound that might have started as a chuckle but became a cough. Clearly, West was bleeding in his lungs.

"I'm telling you this because I want you to know they've got you nailed. If I take off your cuffs, it's no good trying to kill me and get away. You understand that."

Chee still had the keys in his right hand. He had held them there since extracting the ring from the trunk lock and unlocking the front door of the car.

"Lean the other way, toward the other door, and hold out your hands."

West breathed, bubbling, gasping.

"Lean," Chee said. "Hold 'em out."

West leaned, laboriously. Chee leaned the other way, fumbling behind him, finding West's strong hands, finding the lock. Fumbling the key into it, getting—finally—the handcuffs opened and West's hands out of them.

But West had fallen against the passenger-side door now.

"Come on, West," Chee said. "You're loose now. You got to start the engine, and drive us to get help. If you don't, you're going to bleed to death."

West said nothing.

Chee reached behind his back, pulled West straight. West

212

fell against the door again, coughed feebly.

Chee gave up. "West," he said. "How did you manage the business with the squash blossom necklace turning up at Mexican Water? That was a mistake."

"Friend of mine did it for me. Navajo. Owed me some favors." West coughed again. "Why not? Looked like it could confirm Musket was still alive."

"Your friend picked a girl out of the wrong clan," Chee said. He wasn't sure West was hearing him now. "West," he said. "I'm going to have to leave you here and see if I can get help."

West breathed. "Okay," he said.

"One thing. Where'd you hide the rest of the jewelry?"

West breathed.

"From your burglary. When you faked the burglary. Where'd you hide the jewelry that's missing? Lots of good people would like to have their stuff back."

"Kitchen," West said faintly. "Under the sink. Place there where you can crawl under to fix things."

"Thanks," Chee said. He pushed the car door open and swung his legs out, and leaned far enough forward to get his weight on his feet. He lost his balance and sat down again. He was aware that he was used up, exhausted. And then he was aware that West, leaning against the door behind him, was no longer breathing.

After that there was no hurry. Chee rested. Then he reached clumsily behind him and felt the pocket of West's jacket. He worked his fingers into it and extracted a soggy mass of little envelopes. His fingers separated them. Thirteen. One for each card in a suit of cards. Arranged, Chee was sure, so that West's nimble fingers could quickly count inward to the three of diamonds. Or if the seven of clubs was called for, perform the same magic in whichever pocket stored the clubs. But West's illusions were all ended now. Chee had another problem. He remembered Captain Largo, grim and angry, ordering him to stay away from this narcotics case. He imagined himself opening the trunk of his patrol car and confronting Largo with a suitcase full of cocaine—seventy pounds of evidence of his disobedience. A scene worth avoiding. Chee listened to the rain and decided how this avoidance could be accomplished. Then he let his thoughts drift to Miss Pauling. She, too, had gotten her revenge. West had killed her brother to make it possible to revenge himself. And now her brother, too, was revenged. At least, Chee thought he was. It wasn't a value taught, or recognized, in the Navajo system and Chee wasn't sure he understood how it was supposed to work.

Finally he pushed himself to his feet again, and walked to the car trunk, and managed, with his cuffed hands, to get the second aluminum suitcase shut again, with the broken catch holding. He eased it out of the trunk and down the slippery, rain-washed rocks toward Polacca Wash. The water was higher now, lapping against the first suitcase. Chee gave that one a hard shove with his foot. It floated briefly and then was sucked down into the boiling current. He spun around then, and sent the second case spinning after it. When he turned to look, it had already been lost in the darkness.